KU-862-938

WINNERS

Mary-Ellen Lang Collura

CANONGATE · KELPIES

First published in Canada in 1984
by Western Producer Prairie Books, Saskatchewan
First published in Great Britain in 1988 under the title *Jordy*
by Spindlewood, Barnstaple
First published by Canongate Kelpies in 1990

© 1984 by Mary-Ellen Lang Collura

Cover illustration by Linda Herd

Printed and bound in Great Britain
by Cox and Wyman Ltd, Reading

ISBN 0 86241 295 1

CANONGATE PUBLISHING LTD
17 JEFFREY STREET, EDINBURGH EH1 1DR

To Margaret Gourley, Oshawa

One

JORDY THREEBEARS SLOUCHED IN HIS SEAT at the back of the bus and closed his eyes. He was only fifteen, but already he'd seen enough of Alberta to last a lifetime. Eleven foster homes in eight years, and moving again. It was enough to make him sick.

The social worker sitting beside him stirred in his sleep and twitched. Jordy edged closer to the window, away from him. Social workers, especially Mr. Hagel, made him sick too. Bunch of useless busybodies, picking into his head, bouncing him around the province whenever they felt like something to do. He could do without them. He longed to be free, unbothered by rules, schools, and grownups telling him what to do. He opened his eyes briefly and noticed a cowboy out on the plains, riding a horse over a little hill towards the first rays of autumn sunlight. The image stayed in his mind as the bus rumbled on towards Calgary—a rider and his horse, running across the prairie. That would be freedom.

Mr. Hagel twitched again, woke up, and rubbed his eyes. "Guess I was dreaming," he muttered and settled back into his seat. Dreams! Jordy snorted. He could do without them. Already he had learned life was easier to take if you didn't have dreams.

He closed his eyes, tried to block out everything. The years of moving from place to place amounted to a blur with only an occasional clear memory. He remembered the little girl in the first foster home, and how she used to follow him around. He remembered Mr. White, a P.E. teacher in a town he couldn't recall, yelling for the world to hear, "Nice move Jordy! You could be a gymnast!"

1

The face of a judge peering down at him and saying, "We have decided to place you in a new foster/home," was also clear in his mind. But not much else.

Jordy rammed his fists into the pockets of his jacket, opened his eyes, and clenched his teeth. Ahead, he could see the lights of Calgary. He thought about who was waiting there. The social worker had been so pleased and excited when he had told Jordy the news. "Going home to your grandfather, after eight years away." Even now Jordy did not know what to feel about this. Home meant where you slept, that was all. And grandfather? The father of a parent, someone connected by blood. At first the news had struck him like a surprise, something between the surprise of a Christmas parcel and a razor blade in a hallowe'en apple. Now he could summon only fear. Someone claimed him, someone he didn't know wanted to take him to a place he couldn't remember.

It was dawn. A swath of yellow highlighted the space between the awakening earth and the vanishing blue-black night. Ahead, he could see the twinkling lights of Calgary, the approaching cars, and the soft splashes of neon signs: Eat Here, Gas, Welcome, Come Again. Jordy felt his stomach growl; whether from nerves or hunger he wasn't sure. He'd be glad when this meeting was over.

The bus slowed as it moved into the city. The wide streets were lined with neat little houses and neat little trees. From his window he could see the houses coming to life as the dawn broadened and brightened into day. A dog barked. A door opened. Nice little town. Nice little lives. Going right by him.

At last the bus turned and cruised into the station. Jordy squinted to see better, but there was no sign of anyone who looked like a grandfather. The knot in his stomach crawled up to his throat. He gulped. The bus groaned and hissed to a stop. Passengers stood up and filled the aisle as they groped for belongings and bumped their way to the door.

"Let's go," Mr. Hagel said. He planted a hand in the middle of Jordy's back, propelling him forward.

Jordy wrenched himself out of reach of the hand and sauntered to the front of the bus and down the few steps with a spring in his step and the touch of a swagger in his shoulders. But when he reached the cold grey pavement he paused and took a breath. For once his anxiety shone through his eyes, betraying him. He looked past the crooked line of departing backs, through the big glass doors of the ticket office, and there they were, an old man and another man. With Mr. Hagel at his side, Jordy walked through the doors and stopped in front of them.

The Department of Indian Affairs man stepped forward and cleared his throat. He held out his hand, first to Mr. Hagel, then to Jordy, shook vigorously, and began. "Yes, well, how do you do? I'm Jeffrey Campbell. Did you have a good trip? So nice to see you. How are you? Yes, well, my, come over here, yes that's right and ah, meet Mr. Speckledhawk, ah, your grandfather, Jordy, that's right, just step over here . . ."

Mr. Speckledhawk held out a hand to Jordy. The strength of his grasp surprised the boy and made him feel better. The two looked at each other, released their hands, looked away. What Jordy had seen was a little old man wearing short little braids. This intrigued him. What the grandfather had seen was the living image of his daughter. This shook him.

The two government men hustled Jordy and his grandfather into the waiting car. Except for Mr. Campbell, who chattered about Calgary and the weather, no one spoke all the way to the Indian Affairs office.

In the office Mr. Campbell sat back in his chair and surveyed his coup. He congratulated himself. Who else would have thought to pair up a man convicted of manslaughter with a borderline juvenile delinquent. He had made it happen. Now he must make it work. He scanned the files before him.

Jordy watched Mr. Campbell's eyes as they skipped over his records. He could imagine what was in these records. "Jordy is bright enough but . . . Jordy ran away again . . . Jordy doesn't try . . . If only Jordy would . . ." He had heard it all a thousand times. Still, he had never gotten used to those withered little judgments everyone stuck on him. His lips curled in a sneer. He noticed, however, as Mr. Campbell began his recitation, that there was no hint of disapproval on his face.

Mr. Campbell began: "In response to the Blackfoot community's expressed determination to take responsibility for its own absent young people, indeed, all its people, this department has begun a program of reunion, where possible, of band members who, for one reason or another, have been placed outside the jurisdiction and direction of their own people. Now, in this particular case, Jordy, you were placed in homes off the reserve because both your parents were dead and no other family member was in a position to take care of you. And, well, to be truthful, the department at that time made a habit of routinely moving Indian youngsters to situations within the broader Canadian community. Well, anyway, times change."

He chuckled into the air and looked over the downcast head of the old fellow and the stare of the young one. He carried on.

"So Jordy, when we were informed that your grandfather was to be released, we approached him about you. We held meetings, made arrangements, and, well, here you are." Mr. Campbell droned on about progress, keeping in touch, and the importance of family ties, but Jordy had stopped listening. Behind the level stare he trained on Campbell, he was thinking about the horse and rider he had seen from the bus window. He wondered what it was like to be free like that.

At last Mr. Campbell finished his speech, all the files were exchanged, hands were shaken, good-byes said, and Jordy and his grandfather got into the old man's truck. The truck belched, lurched, and skidded away from the downtown office. Finally the two were alone together.

On the road east out of Calgary, Jordy looked over at his grandfather and asked, "Where we goin'?" It was as if he had not spoken. The old man kept his eyes on the road.

The boy took his first thorough look at his grandfather. The old face was lean and creased in the usual old-face places. The nose was fine and straight, the chin square, the eyes narrow and dark. Jordy imagined his grandfather's profile bordered with feathers, with about ten years of sun and hard weather added to it, looking like something out of an old West painting. Except for the braids. Jordy guessed they were a recent addition. They didn't look like the product of a lifetime. The old man turned and looked at his grandson.

"Call me Joe," he said.

"Oh."

"And another thing."

"Yeah?"

"When we get to my place, you look out for yourself."

They drove on in silence. Jordy watched the country unfold as the truck wheezed along. They passed miles of range, stands of aspen, little creeks meandering through reddish rock, clusters of houses and trailers, a town, and everywhere, the undulating plains.

Sixty miles east of Calgary, they took a turnoff past Glendon that brought them to a narrow road and the sign beside it that read:

Ash Creek Blackfoot Reserve

No Trespassing

There it was, Jordy's first look at 'home'.

Two

JORDY SAT UP STRAIGHT, all senses alert as they drove through the reserve. To him it didn't look much different from country they'd just come through, except that there were no billboards, no gas and grocery truckstops, and fewer fences. It surprised him though, when they rumbled over the brow of a hill and the road straightened out to become the main street of a little community.

Main Street was bracketed at either end by white men's institutions—a post office, and in the distance, a school. In between, the Blackfoot sense of style prevailed. The houses along Main Street were painted in bright tones of green, orange, red, and aqua blue. Halfway along the street squatted the chief's general store. Albert Greenshoots' Store, with its flagpole and railed front porch, was clearly the center of Main Street.

Jordy's first impression of his reserve was mixed. On the one hand he was amazed to be where nearly every face he saw was Indian. On the other hand, the Indianness all around him made Jordy feel oddly out of place, like an outsider. He didn't know these people; he didn't know the customs, the lingo, the habits of mind and manner that made them a cohesive group of human beings. He didn't know that Jenny Greyhorse who leaned on the railing as she fingered her grocery bag, had been his mother's best friend, and had been dawdling around the store all morning waiting for Joe and his grandson to go by. He didn't know that the Ash Creek Elementary School was having its longest recess of the year because Marabel Hind, who had taught there for twenty-nine years, hoped to catch a glimpse of him. When the pulse of the street missed a beat as he went by, he couldn't see it. All he saw was a small-town street with buildings and trucks in various states of decay or repair, old women and skinny dogs poking in and out around the edges of the houses, clotheslines sagging in the October cold, and smoke pencilling up from the chimneys. It all seemed strange to his city-bred eyes.

Joe Speckledhawk knew his Main Street neighbors were curious about his grandson but he didn't care. Let them peek and wonder. It made no difference to him. He was saddled with this kid to raise and he aimed to do it his own way. Although he'd never sat at home and raised a kid before, he'd been in prison long enough to have learned a lot about what makes people tick, and he figured he could bring up this boy right enough to give him a running start.

Joe lost himself in memories. He thought of his daughter. Jordy's presence had brought her back to him. His beautiful daughter. Any time he was home from the rodeo circuit she was there, eager to bounce on his knee, and as she had grown older, to lightly clasp his arm with a long, tapered hand. He had always been proud of her, her bright wit and her shining eyes. She had done so well in school, she was going to be a teacher, and he'd bragged about her in every diner and bar from here to Moose Jaw. But then he had made a big mistake. Even now he hated thinking about it. He had brought that bum back with him from the Chilcotins. Henry George Threebears. Handsome bastard. Bright black hair and flashing white smile. When he got her letter from Cache Creek saying she was married, she was happy, she was sorry, he'd wanted to crush her he was so angry. Sarah, running off with a rodeo bum. The thought of it had nearly killed him. But when he got her other letter saying Henry was dead, she was pregnant, please could she come home, he had dropped all his fury like a stone, opened his heart to her again, received her with joy. Those had been good years, his house filled with her and her little son. He had boasted of them right across the North American rodeo tour.

He pulled his mind out of his reverie. He didn't want to think of the rest. His life had died with hers that night, his body had been swallowed by the grey monster prison, and if there was any life for him now, he had not yet claimed it.

He drove straight through Main Street out to the other side of town and turned the truck left off the road. The old truck bounced and clattered across rough prairie, over a hill, down to a grove of trees by a creek, and straight through a stand of cottonwoods. There it screeched to a halt beside a cabin in a meadow.

Jordy got out of the truck and looked around. Behind him was the grove of trees. To his right he could see the edge of the cut the creek made in the prairie. To his left rose a curving hill. All around him waved the burnished autumn grasses. The cabin was a prefabricated aluminum building. Beside it squatted the well. Behind it tilted an outhouse. Being out in the middle of the prairie, there were neither power lines nor sewage system. No TV, no phone, no toilet, no furnace. Jordy groaned inside himself. He wasn't going to like this, he was sure.

It was like moving from one century to another to walk from the aluminum exterior of the cabin to the interior. Jordy stopped in surprise. Joe had hung the inside walls with hides and skins, beaded pouches, rattles with feathers drooping from them, a drum and a quiver and an unstrung bow. The effect was to produce warmth in contrast to the cold shiny siding on the outside. The room seemed like the inside of a tipi. The soft pops and crackles in the woodstove in the center of the room with its scent of hemlock and birch seemed to blend with the brown and grey softness of the walls.

Joe was not used to explaining himself. However, as he eased past Jordy standing in the doorway and went to stoke the stove he said, "This here's how I like it, away from everyone. Don't need to worry about bills and sewer lines here."

Jordy looked from the walls to his grandfather. He didn't know what to say.

"It okay with you?" Joe asked.

"Sure. I guess."

In fact, nothing was particularly okay with Jordy at the moment. He was wondering what he'd gotten into. Stuck in the middle of nowhere with this odd old man. No TV. Nothing to do. Nowhere to go. Running away was beginning to look attractive. And yet a little part of Jordy was curious.

Joe showed Jordy his room. It was the back quarter of the cabin partitioned from the rest by skins hanging from a pole. There was a cot, and a chest of drawers beside the window. There was a kerosene lantern hanging over the bed.

Jordy put his suitcase on the bed and stuffed his few things in the drawers. Joe showed him the rest of the place. Joe's bed and workbench were stationed to the right of the front door, the narrow bed against the wall, the workbench beside the front window. Stacked in the corner, a pile of skins and hides teetered within grabbing reach of the workbench. Beneath the table sprawled an assortment of cardboard boxes with sticks and bits of bone poking out of the unflapped tops.

The stove and woodbox stood in the middle of the cabin. The left side of the cabin was the kitchen. The back wall beside Jordy's room contained cupboards, counters and sink, tins of meat, sacks of flour, cups, plates, and pots. Against the front wall were boots, rifles, axes, a shovel, and a sledge hammer. Beneath the window on the side wall stood the kitchen table, a magnificent island of order amidst the clutter surrounding it.

Joe brought out the sugar bowl, a can of milk, and two cups. He poured coffee into the cups and set them on the table. First Joe, then Jordy, sat down. They clinked their spoons, fingered their cups, sipped, and sat.

"Well," said Joe at last.

"Uh huh," Jordy finally answered.

"We gotta talk."

"I guess."

"Mr. Campbell said we should talk."

"About what?"

"I dunno. Maybe get things straight between us."

"Like what?"

"I dunno. You got any questions?"

The truth was Jordy had many questions. But they were very private ones, questions he had never asked anyone, ever. He was afraid of these questions and of their answers. Who was his mother? His father? Who was he? What had happened to them all? Sometimes, thinking about these things twisted up his insides. Sometimes, he merely acknowledged them, sitting inside him, an unfortunate backdrop to the steps and turns of his life.

Jordy shifted in his chair. He looked out the window to the hillside. He felt far away from everywhere. Then, yes, he had a question.

"What about school?"

"What about it?"

"How'm I goin' to get there?"

"Bus takes Indian kids into Glendon from Main Street. Not many go past grade seven."

"How do I get to the bus stop?"

"Walk."

"Oh."

Which would be worse, dragging himself off to school or hanging around here? At that moment, Jordy felt in favor of school. At least there'd be something familiar going on.

Three

AS NOVEMBER UNFOLDED, JORDY DECIDED that life on the reserve with his little grandfather was no big deal. The reserve was just a boring sprawl of prairie, and Joe just a solemn old man who didn't bug him.

At first, Jordy had waited for some sign, some recognition that they were a family. But as the weeks went by and Joe maintained an unobtrusive distance, Jordy gave up waiting. Apparently the way white folks behaved in their homes was not the way Joe Speckledhawk would behave in his.

School had some problems.

First, there was getting there. Jordy was not used to getting out of bed at 5:00 A.M. Nor was he used to braving subzero winds, sleet, or snow on the open plains and in the dark. It made him feel alone and small to be hiking across trackless expanses of wind-washed prairie, the sparkle of receding stars a counterpoint to the sudden shadows and streaks of emerging daylight, the little hoots and rustles of unseen creatures skittering away from his approach.

Still, Jordy cherished the notion that he was tough and he made himself stride out to brave whatever was on this alien landscape that might test him. And there was something exhilarating about filling his lungs with cold air, about meeting the sun rising, and feeling his blood rush through him as he walked. Although he never liked getting out of his warm bed and gulping his gritty coffee in the dark, he took pride in his four-mile trek to the bus pick-up on Main Street.

As for the bus ride, he took no pleasure in it. He didn't like waiting in front of the elementary school with ten other teenagers who made little attempt to get to know him. Not that he made it easy. He hung back from them and did not enter into their bantering. Still, he would have appreciated some gesture on their part acknowledging some common bond between them. Or something.

Nor did he like the bus. Ugly old rattletrap. It was cold and jarring and gutless. It embarrassed him to be disgorged from its sagging innards in front of a schoolful of town kids who were being dropped off by their parents or by Glendon's new bus.

Jordy was everyone's outsider. The Glendon kids took him for a Reserve Indian, someone to whom they assigned insoluble differences and cultural distances. His fellow Blackfoot students saw no reason to associate with him. He had shared no part of their lives that they could remember. He kept himself apart at school. As always, he was surrounded by masses of strangers rushing past him as he bumped his solitary way through a maze of halls. He made no attempt to get to know anyone.

There were two things in the Glendon Secondary School that he liked. The Physical Education teacher was a person whose energy and enthusiasm had drawn Jordy to her, rekindled the athletic spark in him that had occasionally been fanned before. Jane MacTavish could see that Jordy was a natural and talented athlete. The fact that Jordy was still small for his age was not, in his case, a handicap. He was quick, co-ordinated, and able to out-maneuver his bigger classmates. He was strong and supple and possessed the grace of a dancer. He worked hard in her class and sometimes helped her move equipment.

The second attraction was the Junior Rodeo Association which the school sponsored. Jordy's eyes lit up at the sight of the rodeo posters, the belt buckles and boots worn by rodeo riders in school. Those riders seemed to project an aura of self-confidence that Jordy envied. He longed to be a rodeo man, have a horse.

But the only time he'd mentioned rodeo to Joe, the old man had snorted and turned away. Thus Jordy kept his interest in rodeo to himself. He didn't discuss anything with his grandfather. The old man minded his own business and expected Jordy to mind his.

On the first Monday morning in December, Jeffrey Campbell showed up in the school office to check on Jordy. He was anxious to know how Jordy and his grandfather were getting along and how school was going for Jordy. He was curious about a lot of other things too, but for this first visit those two concerns were enough.

Mr. Campbell was fidgeting with his file folders and chewing the end of his pencil when Jordy sauntered into the room. He rose from his chair in a fluster, banged his knee against the desk as he reached forward to Jordy, clasped his hand and said, "Ah, yes, young man, good to see you, how are you? Well, you're looking well Jordy, yes that's right, sit down, won't you? That's right, how are you? How've you been getting along? Yes, well. Well? How are you?"

"Okay."

"Good! You're looking well. How are you keeping?"

"Okay."

"How do you like school?"

"It's all right."

"Well. Yes. Hmmm. Your attendance is good. Comments from teachers are favorable. Yes, yes, Jordy, you're doing fine. I'm proud of you."

Although Jordy could see no reason why Campbell should be proud of him, he accepted the statement with some gratitude. It felt good.

"But what do you really think of school here?" Campbell prodded. The question was a surprise.

Jordy considered his best move, and then decided to give the truth. He would know from the man's reaction whether Campbell really was all right or not. "It's dumb."

"Oh?"

"But I like P.E. Miss MacTavish is okay. And I like sports."

"Good. Yes. From your reports I can see you've always been a good athlete. Take after your father I suppose." Mr. Campbell chuckled slightly, aware of the surprise in Jordy's eyes. He carried on. "I'm happy to see you're doing so well in P.E. Miss MacTavish says you are a great help to . . ."

"Hey!" Jordy's mind was in a spin. Mr. Campbell knew something about his father.

"Yes Jordy."

"You said something about my father."

"Yes."

"What about him?"

"What would you like to know?"

This was not the right question. Jordy didn't know what he wanted to know. It was too difficult. For too long he had consigned the idea of 'father' to the shadows.

Mr. Campbell could see the tension in Jordy's face. He said gently, "Your dad was a very fine athlete."

"Oh?"

"He was a rodeo star."

"Yeah?" Jordy could feel his heart beating faster.

"Yes. He used to ride the broncs, saddle and bare-back."

"He did?"

"Yes. That's how he died. A bronc fell over backwards in the chute on top of your father. It crushed him against the boards. It was a terrible accident. Your father was a fine athlete, a superior rider."

Jordy's tension vanished. Relief and amazement took turns flying through his head. His father had been a real rodeo man. Jordy smiled.

"He rode the horses, eh?"

Mr. Campbell nodded. "He was very good."

Jordy felt a rush of determination. Before his racing heart could sweep the moment past him, he must ask, he must find out. Years of shadows and whispers might be wiped clear.

"My dad, he . . . she . . . uh, I mean, my mother . . ."

Jordy's face twisted. He tried to bring it to control. He was afraid.

Mr. Campbell leaned forward and said softly, "Your mother was a lovely lady. A winner. She was expecting you when your dad died." He rummaged quickly through his folder until he came to a piece of paper which he scanned briefly, then passed to Jordy.

It was a photocopy of a snapshot. It was pale and blurred but, nonetheless, it showed a happy couple. Their arms were around each other, his sleeves rolled up, her cotton dress waving off to the left in a summer wind, a picnic spread before them, their youth and features crystallized for Jordy on that piece of paper.

Jordy scarcely breathed. He stared and stared at the picture. Two real people, and that's what they had looked like. He could not take his eyes from them.

Mr. Campbell reached forward and patted his shoulder, but Jordy made no move. Mr. Campbell sat back in his chair. He, too, scarcely breathed. At last Jordy looked up.

"My parents look all right," he said.

"I'd say so," replied Mr. Campbell. He grinned. "You look like your mother, Jordy."

"I know," the boy whispered.

Suddenly, he felt an elation so strong he thought he would burst. A rush of energy pounded through him, demanding release. "I gotta do something."

"Sure, go ahead."

"I gotta get out of here for awhile."

"That's okay, Jordy. I'll explain it to the office."

Jordy looked at Mr. Campbell. The man was all right. Jordy said, "Thanks," and ran out the door.

Four

WHEN HE HAD RUN OUT OF TOWN, Jordy let himself fall onto the prairie. He lay on his back, his chest heaving against his zippered jacket, aware of his heart pounding. He listened to it, sounding up from its cavern into his ears. He opened his eyes. Up in the sky there was humming and colors spinning. He took a deep breath, then lay still until the pounding slowed and the colors sank back to earth and the sounds around him died.

Jordy thought about the picture of his parents. A laugh came tripping up into his throat. He opened his mouth and it sparkled out through his teeth, out across the air like pebbles clinking down copper piping.

He knew who he was. Everything was clear now and the world was brand new. His father was a star. His mother was a winner. He had been a rodeo man. She had been beautiful. Imagine if they had lived, where he'd be now. He would be the junior rodeo champion of North America. Everyone would know who he was. He would be a rider above the walkers. A winner.

He sat up and looked around. Stillness surrounded him. He got up, rubbed his arms and stamped his feet. He was cold.

He found the road, and as he walked back towards Glendon he thought about the picture. His father's face was round and smooth, his black hair glistening in sunshine, his eyes laughing. His father looked young. Twenty? Twenty-two? The thought of his father being that young gave Jordy a new perspective on fatherhood. He had always thought of fathers as grey and middle-aged, soft and potty or triangular and boney, distant creatures who read papers, did Saturday chores, and intoned the dinner prayers, not people of much consequence.

His father looked strong. His shoulders were broad and his forearms taut and well muscled. The hand around his mother's shoulder was wide and well formed. Jordy tried to imagine how his father must have sounded and how he must have walked. Since he'd been a horseman, he must have been bowlegged, and since he'd been a star, he must have been supple and strong. A man who made heads turn when he moved. In his mind Jordy set this man on a horse and had him ride beside him down the road. This father, the real one, a young, vibrant horseman, kept pace with Jordy into Glendon. A strong, handsome father, someone he could be proud of. Jordy discarded the images of all the other pale old fathers he had ever lived with.

His mother had looked young, not much older than Jordy was now. Mr. Campbell had said she was a winner. What had he meant by that? Joe had said one night, as Jordy sighed over his boring homework, that Jordy's mother had been a very good student. Was that what Campbell meant by a winner? A smart student? Or was there more to it than that?

Jordy knew his mother had died suddenly when he was seven. Something about it had been very terrible, but his mind wouldn't recall what it was. Now, at least he knew she had been beautiful. Seeing her face in the photograph had brought a spurt of impressions to the surface of his mind. He remembered her long, black hair and how she would fling her head back to make it fly out behind her. Sometimes, when he had been little, she had picked him up and danced around the cabin with him in her arms. He could remember the smoothness of the movement; how she had rocked him as she danced; how soft and strong it had felt to be secure inside the circle of her arms; how the window, door, table, and stovepipe had whirled past his eyes as the dance picked up speed; how he had laughed and begged for more.

Jordy lifted his elbows, picked up his feet and began to

jog. He could see the clusters of Glendon houses ahead and the gas station. Just then a bright black truck came screeching out of the gas station, heading towards him. He slowed down, pausing instinctively as he watched the roaring truck come towards him. The truck picked up speed. His nerves tightened. As it streaked towards him he could see the outlines of several men in the cab. Arms waved out the windows, a hand holding a beer bottle shook against the wind. Jordy stopped. The beer bottle hurtled towards him.

He tumbled off the shoulder of the road into the ditch. The bottle whacked him in the back. His heart raced as he gasped for air.

"Damn dirty Indian!" someone shouted.

"Got him!" another bellowed. There was a laugh. The truck tires crinkled over gravel. The muffler belched, then the sounds roared away. Jordy lay still, feeling his heart pounding like a mad drummer. He sucked in air until he stopped shaking, then he rolled over and got up.

Jordy swept the dust and bits of gravel from his clothes. The tightness in his chest hurt. He felt like screaming and he wanted to smash something. But he could only stand and shiver. His jumpy muscles had started to knot and he knew he had to move, so with his head down and his fists clenched he started back to town.

His good feelings had vanished like tumbleweeds blown away in a prairie dust storm. A sense of hopelessness compounded the rage that was welling up in him. What was he after all? He wasn't a rodeo man. He didn't have a mother or father. All he had was a dumb old grandfather who looked ridiculous. He didn't have a friend and he hated school. There was no use to anything. The white world threw beer bottles at him and ran him off the road. The Blackfoot world ignored him. His spirit needed sanctuary, and there was none.

He arrived back at school at lunchtime. The dreary halls were filled with mumbling people and muffled noises, smells of scarves and rubber boots, and around the corner, the mustard and buns air of the cafeteria. He barged through the halls, his head down, his hands knotted, reflections of the knots tightening around his heart and mind. He pushed people out of his way. He wanted a fight. He headed for the gym.

He got there just as Miss MacTavish was taking down the badminton nets. She looked up and greeted him with her usual cheerful "howdy," expecting his usual friendly help. He glared at her and headed for the locker room. The junior boys' basketball team was suiting up for a lunch hour practice. They paid no attention to him and he stormed back out onto the gym floor. He leaned against the wall, his fingers itching for a ball to bounce while his dark eyes watched the boys file out of the locker room. They called to each other and dodged and darted around the supervising teacher as she hauled the clump of netting to the supply room.

Basketballs like bullets fired around the court; bodies and basketballs merged and split apart like machine-gun explosions; rubber-soled skids ricochetted off the waxy floor; and the warm smell of sweat began to percolate through the air.

Suddenly a ball slammed against Jordy's head, the force of it spinning him half around. Jordy exploded. He catapulted himself into the nearest player, drove his head like a ram into the boy's guts, and threw him with a numbing whack onto the cold floor. Then there were elbows and knees and fists all over him, and with each jab and blow, Jordy's strength surged and his fists flailed. He fought like a crazy man.

There was a momentary lull and from above him Jordy heard a voice bellow: "That's ENOUGH! Get up, ALL of you! Jordy Threebears you STOP THAT!"

The elbows and knees unwedged themselves from his body as the boys got up. The fury subsided and there was Jordy standing alone, a ragged curve of red-faced boys behind him, a furious teacher before him. Jordy's chest heaved; he licked at a trickle of sweat dripping down his face. He squared himself and looked at Miss MacTavish.

Her eyes were bright and round, her cheeks flushed. Her voice quavered and her hands shook as she faced them all.

"Jordy, I want you to go to the office. You other boys, I'll see you in the locker room."

"But Miss MacTavish! He . . ."

"No! I don't want to hear it at the moment. You have all acted like barbarians."

"But Miss MacTavish! He started . . ."

"Be quiet! Go to the locker room!"

"But . . ."

"NOW!"

As they shuffled to the locker room the team nonetheless loudly relieved themselves of their collective spleen:

"Bloody redskin . . ."

"We should've killed 'em all a hundred years ago."

"Dumb creep."

"Dirty fighter . . ."

Jordy stood alone in front of Miss MacTavish. He could not look at her.

"What's gotten into you?" she said.

He said nothing. Inside he felt dead.

"Jordy, your behavior was disgusting."

The words burned him. He felt his control crumble. He began to walk away.

"Jordy! I'm talking to you."

His back was to her, shutting her out. He continued walking.

"You're to go to the OFFICE!"

He raised his head. He stared straight ahead and kept walking.

"Jordy? You hear me? You're to go to the office!"

He walked through the school, out the door, away from the town, out toward the open prairie.

Five

JORDY WALKED OUT ONTO THE PRAIRIE with the unsteady
gait of a zombie, his mind blank. On and on he went, until
dusk filtered into the light. Then he lay down in the grass,
curled himself up, and dozed the semisleep of the
despondent. Thus he passed the night, a tight little ball of
humanity, lost and alone, a solitary pinpoint on the wide,
wind-worn prairie.

When the first rays of the morning sun divided the dark,
Jordy got up and walked again. His whole body ached
from the accumulated effects of cold and yesterday's
bruises, but he didn't care. He wished to die. Perhaps then
he would really be with his parents. At least he would be
through with this miserable life.

Sometime in the morning he passed a farm and crossed
a road. Then he came to another farm, then several more.
Dogs barked and cows shied. He kept to the edges of fields
and sat down somewhere during the afternoon and slept.

When he awoke, he heard the nighthawks swooping and
the field mice scurrying. Black shadows fluttered around
him and little rustles sent prickles of fear up his spine.
Everything ached—his bones, his brain, and his stomach
pleaded with him for some solace. He didn't care. It
appeased him somehow that everything hurt.

He felt so cold his lungs ached. He got up and began to
walk, waving his arms, stomping his feet. The cold inside
him was terrible. And it was odd that while his feet felt like
cement blocks being dragged through mud, his head felt
light, as if it were floating from his shoulders. He couldn't
think clearly. What was he doing out here? Where was he?
What had happened? He shook his head from side to side,

then tried to focus his eyes on something. But the shapes attached to the earth waved away from him, shadows rippled past his eyes and into his mind. Nothing was steady.

Finally he fell, exhausted. The smack as he hit the ground jarred his senses. He opened his eyes and saw above him a thousand floating points of light, sailing over him, reaching down to touch him. He raised his head, opened his mouth. The spots reached him, settled their tiny caresses on his face. His brain cleared.

"Snow!" he said.

The sound of his voice startled him. His brain focused. He was lost. He had not eaten for two days. It was cold. It was snowing. He was exhausted. He didn't know which way to go. It occurred to him that he must do something quickly or he would die. He wanted to live; he wanted it so much he felt as though his heart would break.

"No!" he said, in defiance to the cold and the dark and the silent lurking shadows.

Unsteadily, he stood up. Snow spun around his head. He paused, trying to force some calm into his mind. Which direction had he come from? When had he last seen a road or a house? He looked at the ground. Where he had lain, the grass was flat. Where he had walked, the grass had long since unbent itself. He struggled to remember some sign indicating his line of travel, but the snow had obscured it.

Silently, steadily, snow was engulfing him. Nonetheless, stubbornly, Jordy started out.

He lost track of how long he had been on his feet, or where his feet were taking him. He was dimly aware that the world was growing slower and slower, as the snow spun its slow white webs through his head. He was so tired. He ached for rest. He stopped, looked around.

Ahead of him something moved. He squinted. It moved again. A rider? He thought he heard a muffled whinny. He opened his mouth and tried to yell but no sound came. He tried to raise his arms to wave but they would not obey. He felt his heart crying, "Don't leave me out here!" He stumbled forward. The rider moved, beckoned to him, one arm raised in greeting. Jordy called, "Hey! Help!" The silent rider nodded and moved away. Jordy stumbled forward, following.

The horse and rider seemed to float before him. He reached out for them, but clasped only snowflakes. He kept going towards them; they kept retreating. He knew he could not keep on his feet much longer. Then he tumbled down a hill. He staggered to his feet, desperate. Where was his rider? Again, through the dancing snow, he saw them. This time they were closer, their forms were clearer. The horse was grey, small and boney. The rider, only a dark form, barely distinguishable from the horse, wore on his head and down his back a graceful, sweeping trail of feathers. His long black hair rustled slightly against the blanketed shoulders. The black eyes looked deeply into Jordy, the hand beckoned, and Jordy heard a voice say, "Siksika."

"Help me!" he cried. The horse and rider moved steadily on until he could no longer see them. Frantic, Jordy plunged forward.

Up ahead he saw a light. He started to run. The light became clearer. It was square and golden yellow. With his last particle of strength and will, Jordy hurled himself towards a cabin. He stumbled, crashed into the doorway, and then with a sigh, gave in to the darkness.

Six

ERASMUS WATERMEDICINE was a big, stubbly cowboy, gap-toothed and weather-beaten, full of coffee grounds and tall tales. His cabin smelled of saddle leather, horse sweat, and beans; and its owner, of fifty years' accumulation of prairie dirt, sage, and tobacco.

He lived by himself on the MacKenzie ranch, a 130,000 acre sprawl devoted to Hereford cattle and hay. He lived by himself because he preferred the company of the wind and a horse to that of people. He minded only two things —his own business and the business of the ranch. Jacob MacKenzie tolerated old Watermedicine's rent-free outpost because Watermedicine looked out for his cattle. He deterred rustlers, he rescued stray cows and calves, and he rode fencelines. If Watermedicine didn't want to be disturbed, if he just wanted his place to himself and a job by himself, that was okay with MacKenzie.

Erasmus Watermedicine had been a Blood Indian once but he'd given it up. Being this or that made life too complicated, he thought, and he hated complications. As he saw it, there were two kinds of people—honest ones and phonies. Same thing with horses; only with horses, the honest ones far outnumbered the phoney, or bad-hearted types.

In any case, Erasmus made no claims upon his Indian ancestry. He was just himself, unrelated to any of those human institutions into which people are born, and to which he felt they invariably cling throughout their lives. Family, race, religion, culture, politics, none of them held any attractions for him. He was content to eat and sleep and breathe, watch the wind sweep around him, smell the rain and the earth, see the sky move, and the wild horses run. He was quite happy in his solitary way.

Every season had its attractions for Erasmus. He loved the starkness of winter, the gushing revival of spring, the heat of summer, and the ripeness of fall. Now that winter had come, Erasmus was peacefully settling into its routine. He took particular joy in winter nights, snug in his warm cocoon, relishing his solitude while outside his walls, the wind wailed and the snow drove itself against his door. On this night he had come in from checking a small herd of cows, bedded down his horse, fired up his stove, and settled down to a blistering cup of coffee. He sipped it slowly, noisily, feeling the heat trickle down his throat.

He heard a muffled whack against his door, then a cry like that of a wounded rabbit. He rushed to the door and pulled it open. Cold smacked him in the chest, snow blew in his face. He looked down, stunned to see what looked like a heap of clothes flung in his doorway.

On his knees he peered, nose to nose, into the face of a half-frozen boy. The kid was mumbling and moaning. Erasmus pulled him inside, took off his frozen outer clothes, rubbed him to get a little warmth going inside him, wrapped him in a blanket and propped him in a chair beside the woodstove. Then he tried to get some hot coffee down the boy's throat.

Slowly, the boy tossed his head from side to side. Erasmus held his jaw in one hand, pried open his mouth with the other, and tipped in a little of the liquid heat. The boy spluttered and sneezed. Erasmus tried again, then gave up.

The boy was shaking. Erasmus picked up his feet and rubbed them between his own sandpaper-rough hands. The feet didn't look too healthy. In fact, neither did the rest. The hands were blue, the face looked blotchy. Frostbite, probably pneumonia, thought Erasmus. He knew he was going to have to stay with this kid.

His first line of thought was methodical and logical. If the kid had been a horse, he'd have to do things gradually.

Quick temperature changes are deadly for horses, he reasoned, and the same must be true for any warm-blooded creature.

He got a bucket and melted some snow in it. When the water was warm, he put the boy's feet in it, and then he added hot water, a cup at a time. He wrapped the boy's head in a towel and rubbed his back briskly. After awhile he managed to pour some coffee down the boy's throat.

The boy moaned. Erasmus began to hum in soft low tones as if quieting a frightened horse. The boy's eyes opened, shut again, and his head rolled back.

"Mama! Mama!"

Erasmus shook his head and bent close to the boy's ear. "Hey, kid," he said, "I ain't yer Ma. I'm Erasmus. I'm going to put you to bed now so you'll be warm. And when you've had a rest, yer sense'll come back to you. . . . Damn well better, anyhow."

He bundled the boy into his cot which he had moved close to the stove. He sat down in his chair beside him. Outside, the wind whipped itself against the cabin and drove a wave of sleet against the windows. The boy shook at the sound and cried out, "Mama!" His eyes were open, round and staring. He sat up in bed, stretched out his arms to the empty air.

Erasmus put his arms around the boy and held him while the eyes stared and the lips murmured over and over in broken tones, "Mama, Mama." This gave way to ramblings and exclamations. Erasmus could make out the words "dad" and "rider" and once, to his surprise, the word "Siksika." Then he cried out once clearly, "Wait for me! Don't leave me alone!"

The boy stopped shaking, sank back into the pillow, and closed his eyes in sleep. Erasmus went back to his chair, propped his head against his hand, and dozed. The wood fire hissed and popped.

A long-locked door had opened in Jordy's mind. The hidden memories, the horror, the sorrow, had been released. Finally, clearly, he remembered what had happened to his mother.

She had gone to a dance. After the dance, something had made her die. Something had made grandfather rage and wail and kill someone. The impressions of his seven-year-old self were no clearer than this. But one stunning memory was mercilessly clear—his mother dead, her face immobile in the casket, her hands cold, the coldness when he touched her face. He was appalled; this could not be believed. And no one to help him, a house full of strangers, grandfather gone, whispers all around him, his head patted by hands he did not know. And mama. She should come home and make all this go away. She should be herself again, not that cold form in a box. It was all too terrible.

From then on he had been abandoned. He had been alone among strangers all those years. Until now. They had come back to him, he had seen them, his father riding with him through the snow, his mother in her cotton dress speaking to him in this cabin.

Erasmus stirred in his chair and looked at the boy. His face was peaceful. The kid seemed okay, but Erasmus knew trouble could crop up yet. He looked outside. The storm had passed; the sky was clear and beginning to brighten.

He rummaged through one of the boxes in a corner and pulled out a pot and a bag of rolled oats. He made a watery gruel and dumped a glug of syrup into it. This ought to fill out the kid's innards a bit, he thought. No telling when he's last eaten. Erasmus knew an empty stomach could play a lot of tricks on a person, make eyes see things that weren't there, ears hear sounds that had no source.

He waited until daybreak. He took the porridge to the sleeping boy, gently shook him until his eyes opened, and slipped a spoonful of gruel between his lips. The boy swallowed a few mouthfuls, then turned his head to signify he had had enough. Erasmus bent closer to him.

"Hey," he said. "You there?"

Jordy looked at the man, feeling puzzled. Where was he? Who was this?

"I'm Erasmus. You arrived with the storm. How'd you get here?"

Jordy focused on the face before him. He looked a long time at everything around him. Then he said, "I'm alive."

"Yeah. Well you damned near weren't when I got you. Boy, I never seen the like. What were you doing out there in a storm like that?"

"I got lost."

"How the hell did you get here?"

"The rider—"

"I can tell you something for sure, boy, there's no riders out in storms like that."

"I saw him."

"Sure you did."

Time for more food. Erasmus tucked a few mouthfuls down Jordy's throat, then gave him some coffee, liberally laced with syrup and rum. Jordy made a face.

"You drink it anyway, boy. Got to stay warm inside. What's yer name?"

"I'm Jordy Threebears."

Erasmus's eyes widened in brief surprise. "I got to get you home," he said. "Where's that?"

Jordy's consciousness was not altogether returned to the present. Where was home? The thought of home brought to mind an image of tamarak trees beside a yellow cabin with blue lace curtains, his mother's face vague through the curtains.

"Where d'you live, boy?"

"Uh . . . I live . . . I live on the Ash Creek Reserve with my grandfather, in the middle of a field I guess." This struck Jordy funny and he chuckled. Erasmus eyed him cautiously.

"Well kid, reckon I know your grandfather," he said. "When yer settled and all warmed up, I'm goin' to ride for help. I can likely get a rescue crew out here. I don't exactly know what to do with you."

When Erasmus left to get help, Jordy sank back onto the cot. The fire crackled and beamed its heat out through the grill. He was so tired and weak he could hardly keep his head up. He closed his eyes and drifted back into sleep, a sleep so deep and sound he knew nothing else until the whir of helicopter blades woke him.

The medics strapped him snugly in a stretcher, and he was hoisted up into the bright winter sky in a silver cradle that dangled beneath the rescue helicopter.

Seven

JORDY STAYED IN THE CALGARY GENERAL HOSPITAL four days. He had pneumonia and frostbite. For once, at least, he did not feel alone. His visitors amazed him. There was a steady line of them although he hadn't expected anyone.

The first was Mr. Campbell. Wednesday evening he bustled through the door, one hand fidgeting with his half-open briefcase, the other trying to straighten his tie. He swept into the chair beside Jordy's bed, dropped the briefcase, and as he bent over its scattered papers and stuffed them back into its yawning insides, began: "My dear Jordy, we were so worried, we didn't know where you'd gotten to, and then that storm, it was amazing how you found Mr. Watermedicine's place in the middle of a blizzard, we're so glad you're safe, my goodness . . ." And on and on he went while Jordy let his attention drift.

Suddenly Jordy interrupted. "I remember a lot of things now," he said.

"Oh? What things?"

"About my mother."

"Oh."

"Pow. There it was. I remembered."

"May I help you with any of it?" As he said this, Mr. Campbell ceased his fidgeting, took a deep breath.

"Yeah. Some things I don't understand."

"Well, tell me. I'll try to help."

Jordy looked directly at his visitor. He had a courage now he'd never had before. He felt a new strength inside him.

"I want to know what made my mother die."

Mr. Campbell did not answer for awhile. Finally, very

quietly, he leaned forward and said, "Jordy, you know there are all kinds of people in the world."

"Sure."

"So you know there are hateful people, people who hate whoever's different. Some people hate fat people, or smart people, or Communists, or Liberals, or people of another race."

"Yeah."

"Well," he paused a long time, stared out the window, "most people do all this hating out of ignorance. They just don't know any better, and they've never learned, or tried to think through the ignorance, to see the reality of things, the other side of things. The hatred is bad, but the ignorance it comes from is just, well, human."

"Oh."

"I'm saying this because in a way, it was ignorance that killed your mother—people hating without reason."

He paused again, took a look at Jordy. The boy's sunken eyes stared wide at him from a face almost as white as the pillows holding it up. Campbell's hands were sweating, and he wiped them on his knees.

"Well, Jordy. Your mother went to a dance in Glendon. At the dance some drunken men began to bother her. She slapped one of them and then left. As she was walking on the road to home, these guys jumped out of a truck and began to beat her up. Somehow she got away and ran. They couldn't find her. She wasn't found until the next day. By then she was dead. She'd got a crack on the back of her head and it had killed her. Whether the bang on the head was from a fall or the beating was never clearly established."

He looked at the boy's face. It was still and hard. "Jordy?"

"Yeah?"

"Please tell me what you're thinking."

He was trying to imagine someone attacking his mother. He could feel his heart contract into a hard, tight ball.

"I don't know," he finally whispered.

Jordy didn't remember the rest of Mr. Campbell's visit. He was so tired.

He woke in the early morning to the sounds of cushioned shoes padding along the silent halls, a trolley of trays and pills discreetly jiggling somewhere, muted bells binging over the P.A. system while quiet voices calmly called, "Emergency, emergency." Nurses came and went, checking him over with their professional eyes. Breakfast came and went. He paid no attention. A gang of creeps had killed his mother. He could hardly breathe. He couldn't eat. He mostly slept.

He eventually woke to the touch of his grandfather's hand on his forehead. He opened his eyes, and there was the old man's face close to his, looking at him sadly.

"Oh. Hi," Jordy said.

"Hi." Joe moved back quickly and sat down.

The two sat quietly together for a long time, each locked in his separate sorrow, staring at different corners of the room. A nurse rustled into the room, her starched white crispness breaking the silence between them. After she'd left, Joe shifted in his chair, looked at Jordy, and said, "Bull," through a little chuckle.

"Huh?"

"Bull. Nurses. Lotta busybodies."

"Oh?"

"Yeah, I spent a lotta time in hospitals, bustin' up one thing after another. Rodeo'll do that to you. Nurses always poke ya where ya hurt."

"Yeah."

Again silence fell between them. Since Joe was studying his boots, Jordy turned and stared at him. For once, the old man looked interesting.

"You like horses, Joe?" he finally ventured.

"Yeah."

"I'd like to have a horse."

"Okay."

"Okay?"

"Sure. What sort of horse?"

"I don't know. A good one I guess."

"You know what makes a good one?"

"No."

"Heart."

"Heart?"

"Yeah. A horse that would die under ya rather than quit trying."

"Oh."

"I had a horse like that once. He could go for days, coverin' ground with that big, steady stride he had."

"I'd like a horse like that."

"Yeah?"

"I'd like to ride on the prairie, go as far as I could."

"Uh huh."

When the visitor's hour was over, Joe left to seek out Erasmus. Jordy sat up, and for the first time, missed someone. His grandfather was his family. His. The newness of this feeling was like a distant, just-born star, brightening the interior of his unhappy heart with a small but steady light.

Jenny Greyhorse came to see him that evening. She peeked around the corner into his room and was startled to see him looking her way.

"Oh!" she said. "Hi."

"Hi?"

"Can I come in?"

"I guess so."

She glided into the room and perched on the edge of the chair by his bed. She looked around and took off her hat. Her mass of Afro curls went boing the instant it was released from the hat. It startled Jordy. She giggled and pulled out a pack of cigarettes.

"Mind if I smoke?"

"No."

She lit one. The smoke billowed out of her mouth and curled a hazy wreath around her head. She settled back into her chair and squinted at him.

"Boy! You sure look like your mother," she said. Jordy said nothing. She puzzled him.

"Who are you?" he finally asked.

"Oh, jeez. Sorry. I'm Jenny. I was best friends with your mother. I've always had this idea you are almost my kid, I mean since your mom and I were so close, you know?"

"Oh."

"Or I should keep an eye out for you now that you're back, something like that. You know what I mean?"

"Sort of."

"Well listen. I got a houseful of kids at home. Six of 'em. Youngest is two. Oldest is twelve. Maybe sometime you come over for dinner?"

"Sure."

"Okay. I just wanted to meet you and let you know I was around and interested in you. That all right?"

"Yes."

She asked him all the usual questions visitors ask patients in hospitals. They discussed the weather and Christmas. When it was time to leave, she put on her hat and patted his shoulder.

"See you," she said. She winked.

"Sure," he smiled.

After she had left, he lay back and closed his eyes. It intrigued him to think of this frizzy-haired lady in the same breath as his mother. Jenny seemed very different from anything he had imagined about his mother. Did his mother giggle and smoke? Did the two of them walk the same halls, sit in the same classrooms as he did now, whispering and passing notes? He decided he would visit her.

Some kids from the Reservation Express, as the Blackfoot schoolbus was nicknamed, came to see Jordy the next day. Everyone was awkward and shy and the meeting was mainly characterized by pauses and averted eyes. Nonetheless, it was a start. At least he knew their names now.

Mr. Campbell and Joe came together once. Joe talked

about rodeo, and Campbell talked about fishing. Jordy loved it.

The night before he was to go home, Jordy was surprised to see Miss MacTavish. A timid smile briefly touched her face as she stood just inside the door.

"Hi," she said.

"Uh, hi."

"How are you feeling?"

"Oh, okay I guess."

"I brought some work from school, things to catch up on before you come back in January."

She shuffled the papers she held, and shifted from one leg onto the other.

"You know Jordy, I'm sorry about how things were that day in the gym. I didn't know what was happening with you. I'm sorry."

Jordy was amazed. He was sure she must hate him after what he'd done in the gym. "I'm sorry too," he said. "I was havin' a bad day."

MacTavish relaxed and sat down. She showed him the assignments his teachers had sent and gave him the books he needed.

"Seems like a lot of work to dump on you all at once," she said. "Don't worry about it. When you're feeling better, do as much as you can. Okay?"

"Yeah." He sighed.

"Maybe in the spring you could try out for baseball. I love baseball. We usually field a good team."

"Aw, I don't know." After a long, awkward pause he said, "I like horses."

"You do? I like horses too. I used to ride a lot." She grinned, and her eyes sparkled. "I used to go in races."

"Yeah?"

"Long races. The best horse I ever had could do fifty miles in under four hours."

"You're kidding."

"No. I loved it."

He could think of nothing to say about this, and their

conversation shifted to the weather, and school. It wasn't long before she got up to leave. She reached over to him, patted his arm.

"I hope you're well and strong soon. I hope you have a happy Christmas."

"Thanks. You too."

"See you in the New Year."

The next day, Jordy left for home. Released! Free! Newborn, that's how he felt. The cold December air hit him, sending a rush of blood to his cheeks. He was alive. It felt so good he couldn't wait to do something. "Joe," he said as he stepped away from the hospital, "let's do something."

"What?"

"Go for a spin."

"Where?"

"Anywhere. Let's go fast."

"Can't."

"Why?"

"Truck. She's gutless."

"Oh."

"Never mind. We'll try."

They laughed and got into the truck. Its engine rattled to life, its muffler roared, and it skidded away in the winter slush.

Eight

"JOE," SAID JORDY the night before Christmas, "did you really kill someone?"

"Uh huh."

"Are you sorry?"

"No."

Jordy fingered the block of wood in his hands. He turned it over and over, examining its angles. An idea came to him and he began to chip at it with his little knife. He chipped at random, not sure of how to proceed. He wanted a particular shape to emerge but how to get it out into the open was as yet beyond him.

As his knife worked over the wood, Jordy thought about Joe. His grandfather had killed a man, knifed his guts out. Jordy couldn't imagine the quiet little man in his corner with his piles of hides being so furious that he could murder someone.

Joe wasn't sorry. Jordy thought about this. The old man had killed a killer. Was that so bad? Maybe he'd done the world a favor. He had avenged the death of his daughter. Did that make him bad? Jordy couldn't see any badness in him. But they'd put him in jail.

"Joe?" asked Jordy later, "how did you learn to make the old things you make?"

Joe sighed. The boy was full of questions tonight. Perhaps this was just as well. But they were painful to him. He didn't like to think of things he had been haunted by for years. He put down the leather halter he was working on and faced the boy.

"Jordy," he said, "I'm an old man. I can't always say exactly how or when about some things."

"Yeah, but who showed you stuff like you do?"

"I've seen it around. For awhile I had nothing else to do and I taught myself how to put some things together."

"Oh."

The boy looked disappointed.

"Okay, here it is. I didn't know a thing about Indian stuff until I got thrown in the pen. I met this white guy in there. He was an anthropologist. He knew a lot about Indian things. He showed me. I learned about Indian stuff from a damned honky." He snorted in disgust. Then he chuckled. "Oh, hell, Jordy," he said, "the world's all backwards." He sighed again and went back to working on the halter.

The halter. Joe's fingers lingered on it. He turned it around, appraising the craftsmanship. Not bad. Not for a first try anyway. The halter was for his grandson's horse. He'd never made one before. He hoped it would fit whatever horse was being delivered the next day.

He felt a rumble of nervousness in his stomach. He'd not been one to notice Christmas and he felt unsure of himself now that he'd taken steps to celebrate this one.

He thought back to the one vivid memory of Christmas he had. He had been a boy, a lean, tough kid in the lean, tough thirties, and he'd run away from the Indian residential school. As he worked on the halter, his jaw tightened thinking of that school, its rows of hard metal beds, the antiseptic kitchen, the smell of porridge, the rules hanging about the place, the clink the metal spoons made against the china bowls as the rows of silently bobbing heads bent over them. And the drills, the hair clippings and delousing baths, the cardboard shoes, the lonely wind howling through the cracks in the window frames, all of it was a horror, an offence to his spirit. He'd run away. He'd done this for two reasons. First, they had strapped him for speaking the Blackfoot language. Second, he was homesick. So he had run.

He had gotten as far as Calgary and the Salvation Army Center. He had eaten a turkey dinner surrounded by skid row bums and tubercular Indians. Even now he could recall the smell of booze, spittle, and mould that pervaded the place. Christmas! It was a lot of bull and he preferred to ignore it.

But it meant something to Jordy. He had been brought up by white people, and they were great for celebrating it. Christmas was the one time in a year when their withered white souls had any generosity in them, as far as Joe was concerned.

He sighed and put down the halter. He looked over at Jordy and the little heap of chips accumulating on the table beneath his hands. He wondered what had made the boy so suddenly sure that he wanted a horse. Something had happened to him; he wasn't the same kid he'd been before the storm.

He wondered what sort of horse Erasmus would come up with. Not that he was worried. He trusted Erasmus's judgment about horses. Every Indian horseman in the south of Alberta knew that old Watermedicine was the man to consult when the subject was horses. Erasmus knew where the wild horses ran. He knew how to catch them and how to tame them. He could size up a beast in a minute and tell you what it would be good at. He could doctor it and talk to it and tell you what it said. Joe did not doubt that Erasmus would arrive tomorrow with the right one for Jordy.

"Joe," said Jordy, aware that his grandfather was watching him, "why did you grow your hair?"

Joe felt a stab of annoyance. Damn kid. What was he trying to prove? It had not occurred to him that, in this way, Jordy was laying claim to him, and that by possessing a knowledge of his grandfather, he was acquiring a certain knowledge of himself.

"Why d'ya want to know?"

"Oh, just because."

"Well, never mind."

Jordy put down his work. He was tired. He was also a bit depressed. He had always thought the nagging sense of detachment and sadness at Christmas would be cured if only he had some people of his own. But it wasn't so. Tonight he felt alone, not a part of anything.

"Joe," he said, "I think I'll go to bed now."

"Okay."

He went to his room and snuggled deep into his bed. Through the window he could see the moon and stars. If he thought about them very much, he felt very small and insignificant. Compared to the universe he was an ant, a fleeting blink on the eyes of time.

Nonetheless, when he woke up the next morning, he felt refreshed and happy. Christmas morning! A sense of expectancy spread through him and he leaped out of his room, set the fire in the stove, and put the coffee in the pot.

"Merry Christmas, Joe!"

The old man rolled over in his cot. He opened an eye and set himself up on his elbows. He tipped his head to the boy and said, "Merry Christmas to you, too." That was pretty good. Now what?

"I got you a present grandpa."

"You did?"

"Yeah."

"Oh, well let's see it."

Jordy pulled a package from beneath his bed and passed it to Joe who opened it eagerly in spite of his discomfort.

It was a plaid workshirt from the catalogue, special $14.99. Jenny Greyhorse had helped Jordy pick it out and Mr. Campbell had paid for it. Jordy searched his grandfather's face for some sign of approval or pleasure.

"Uh, Jordy . . . that's real nice . . . thanks."

Joe turned his head away and got out of bed. He pulled on his pants and put his new shirt on. Joe made pancakes. He poured extra syrup on them. As the two were finishing breakfast, they heard a holler outside. Through the frosty kitchen window they could see a swirl of powdery snow on the brow of the hill, then the bobbing shapes of ears, heads, and finally bodies weaving and crashing through the snowdrifts. Presently, the bodies became distinguishable. Two horses, one ridden by a large, bundled man, the other led with a rope, were approaching the cabin from the west.

"Well," said Joe, "let's go see." They put on their coats, pulled on their boots, and hurried outside.

The rider was wrapped in coats and scarves from his knees to the top of his head. The only parts of him to be seen were his sparkling eyes. A mitted hand rose to the muffled face and pulled a scarf away. A cloud of misty breath sailed out from the ruddy face as the mouth appeared and spoke.

"Hello kid."

"Hello."

"Hello Joe."

"Hello."

"I brought a horse," said Erasmus.

"Uh huh," said Joe softly.

"A horse? Wow! A horse! For me?" said Jordy.

"Uh huh, of course for you."

The two men grinned. Jordy's heart turned over. He stepped forward to touch the steaming, prancing horses, first Erasmus's and then, with a sense of magic, the other one.

"Is he mine?"

"He's a she," said Erasmus.

Jordy touched the trembling hide of the small speckled grey horse. The horse threw up her head, her ears flattened, and she veered away, her flaring nostrils huffing and snorting, while her eyes popped wide with amazement and fright. Jordy felt his heart race. She pranced and pawed at the end of the lead rope.

"She's a mite wild yet," said Erasmus. "Don't worry. Your grandfather said the right one was to have lots of go. She'll settle."

Joe's practiced eyes checked out the horse his old friend had picked. She was not big and not chunky like the quarterhorses favoured by most of his neighbours. She was so lean her ribs showed. She was tough from a life spent scrounging on the range for every blade of grass and sip of water, running with a wild herd on the alert for danger at every instant. Her head was a mustang's scraggy, coarse head, but her eyes were big and bright, taking in everything. Her bones and joints and hooves were big, and strong as iron. She was deep through the chest and her back was short. When she tucked herself up as she was doing now as she danced at the end of the rope, it was easy to see the power springing from the haunches. It was easy to see she was strong and fit and able to go for miles.

Erasmus clucked to his horse and swung over to the side of Joe's cabin. There Jordy saw brand new tie-up rings anchored into the four-by-fours holding up the place. Erasmus tied the horses to them with deft, quick knots, patted his horse's neck, let his hand rest a moment, testing something Jordy was unaware of. Satisfied, Erasmus walked behind both animals, tapping them as he went. His horse bobbed its head and shifted its weight off a back leg, relaxed. The wild one jerked back and tossed her head, her round eyes rolled backwards, following him. Erasmus chuckled.

"Ah hell," he said. "It takes a little time. She's got to get used to a lot of strange things."

Joe led them into the cabin. The coffee was burnt in the bottom of the pot, smelling up the house with its acrid ash. He swore in annoyance, picked up the smoking pot and handed it to Jordy.

"Clean this damned thing out with snow."

"Well Erasmus," said Joe as Jordy left, "what about this horse?"

"She'll be okay."

"I don't want the kid gettin' busted up."

"There's lotsa ways to get busted up, Joe." Erasmus eyed his friend wickedly. "You should remember."

Joe snorted in disgust. For over forty years, whenever they met, Erasmus found a way of reminding him. A barroom brawl, Joe knocked cold with a broken jaw, Erasmus left standing, laughing.

Well, Erasmus was different now. So was Joe. What couldn't forty years do to you? Yet who would've predicted how life would change them. Erasmus, the swashbuckling brawler turned hermit. And Joe, the wanderer, rooted.

Jordy came in holding the pot before him.

"It's clean," he said, "I'll make some more." He went to the water bucket and scooped up a potful of water. He put in the coffee and stoked the stove, all the while with his back to them.

"Well, what about this horse you got the boy?" said Joe finally.

"Oh, she's a good one."

"Yeah?" Jordy turned to face them.

Erasmus settled back in his chair by the kitchen table. He got out his pipe, lit it, inhaled. A long, slow trail of smoke filtered out from his mouth and drifted up over his head to hang in a line above them. He closed his eyes for a minute, then leaned forward and directed his words at Jordy.

"That horse you got, I been watchin' her a few years. First saw her in the federal park near Banff runnin' in the hills with her ma and a little herd. That was a dodgy little bunch I'm tellin' ya. Saw her a few more times. The herd was always movin' back and forth across the mountains. The ranchers got a few of them for dogfeed I suppose. But she always angled her way outa them problems, I don't know how. She always turned up where the wild horses were runnin'. One year she had a foal by her side. I don't know what became of it. It wasn't around the next year."

"How old is she?"

"Oh . . ." Erasmus took a puff on his pipe and shut his eyes. "I reckon maybe six . . . maybe seven."

"Oh."

"She's young yet kid, don't you worry, just hittin' her prime. Horse ain't grown up 'til it's five or six anyway."

"Oh."

"I'll tell you why I picked her. First, she's smart. Next, she's tough. Last, she's honest." Erasmus settled back in his chair and exhaled a plume of smoke, satisfied with himself.

The coffee was ready. Its aroma mingled with the smells of pipe and wet wool and leather. The two men relaxed over their mugs, content and at ease. No one spoke.

Jordy stood up, suddenly impatient with old-man rhythms. His horse was outside and he wanted to be with her. He pulled on his boots, jacket, and mitts and bolted out the door.

She was standing with her head companionably touching the other horse's neck. At ease like that she looked small and scruffy, not like the god of spirit and fire she had first appeared to be as she pranced in the snow. Jordy walked around her, looking at her from all angles. She was a grey with occasional little spots of white and black freckled along her flanks and rear. From her fetlocks to her knees her legs were black, and so were her mane and tail. She didn't look like any horse he had ever seen and he didn't know whether that was good or bad or anything.

He thought about a name. What did people call horses? Did it make any difference to horses? How did things get names? He supposed he would think of one sooner or later, but nothing came to mind. Whatever name he found, it would have to feel right to him—as if it belonged to her.

He walked up to her. Her body tensed, her head jerked up and back, taking out the slack in the rope. He put his hand up to her face. She tossed it violently away from him and pulled back on the rope, stretching it further, alarm bulging her eyes.

"Hey, horse," said Jordy softly, "don't worry, don't worry." He drew his words out slowly and softly. He talked to her like a mother soothing a frightened child. "There now, easy does it, it's all right, it's aaaalllll riiight," he crooned.

Slowly the tautness of the rope eased. The horse's ears

flicked forward. Although her alertness did not diminish, her alarm did. The rope slackened some more. Jordy slowly raised his hand up to his own head. Then slowly, slowly, he extended it towards her. She snorted at him and backed up quickly, but almost as quickly, she came forward again. She was curious! She lowered her head and stretched her neck towards him as far as she dared, determined to sniff but not to touch. He held his hand still. Her trembling nose investigated. She huffed and tossed her head. He lowered his hand. She eyed him, interested.

"Gooood horse," he whispered. "That wasn't so bad, was it?"

Her ears flicked at every sound he made. The round eyes contemplated this new person frankly. He raised his hand again and calmly aimed it for her neck. The tension returned. The hand moved closer. She tossed her head up and down and pawed the ground but she didn't retreat. The hand reached her neck and touched her hide. The tips of his fingers felt the muscles ripple and quiver at his touch. He stood close to her while she shook with fright.

"Gooood horse . . . you're okay . . . aaalll riiight."

The strength under his fingertips felt like magic to him. He could barely contain his wonder. This creature, come to him out of the snow and cold, was bold and wild and yet she stood beside him, allowed him to touch her. He felt charged with her energy, full of whistling prairie winds and crystal air.

The moment passed. He backed away and left her to resume her rest with Erasmus's horse. He went for a walk over the brow of the hill to think. He had a feeling that for the first time, something wonderful was his. He imagined himself training her and riding her. He walked a long time, travelling in a circle back to the cabin. He felt good.

Later that night, poised at the edge of his room, his eyes on the floor while his grandfather grunted and pulled out bits of hide from a box to stitch, Jordy paused and said, "Uh . . . Joe?" The old man looked up. "I want you to know . . . ah . . . thanks."

Nine

AT SEVEN O'CLOCK THE NEXT MORNING, a modest convoy of trucks materialized in the cottonwood grove by the creek, a carbon monoxide mist pulsing around it as it weaved through the trees. Jordy was outside with his horse, and saw it coming a moment after the horse began to spook. He ran towards the trucks waving his arms.

"Hey! Stop!" he yelled.

The horse was rearing away from the cabin, tossing and pulling on her rope. Jordy stopped, unsure whether to run back to his terrified horse, or on towards the trucks. Then, from inside the lead truck, an arm appeared, waving back the others. The line stopped. Jenny Greyhorse hung her head out of the truck and called.

"Hey Jordy! Hi! Hey! You guys back there, hold up, eh?"

Jordy ran towards her. She grinned at him.

"Hi Jordy. We've come to build you a corral."

"Huh?"

"Yeah." She grinned again. "Your horse needs a place to stay you know. We're goin' to fix you one. That all right?"

"Sure." His eyes brightened. This was something.

A large, lumpy man got out of Jenny's truck. He went back to the other trucks, directing them where to go. Then he came over to Jordy and shook his hand.

"Hello, young fellow," he said. "I'm Albert Green-shoots. We've come to give you a hand."

At that moment, Joe came stumbling out of the cabin in a fury. "What the hell's goin' on here?" he yelled.

"Oh hello, Joe," Albert called.

"What're you doin' here, Albert?" The old man stomped up to Albert, fuming.

"Come to put up a corral for the boy."

"Don't need any damned help."

"You got it anyway," replied the chief.

Joe snorted and shook a fist at the portly Albert. "You got no business bein' here," he said.

"We're here though."

"That horse damn near pulled my house over," Joe fussed. "Least ya coulda done was let me know."

"Where do you want the corral?"

"I was goin' to build it around this stand of cottonwoods."

"Good idea."

"I know that. Don't need you tellin' me."

Joe snorted and stomped off towards his cabin. Men, boys, and girls tumbled out of the assembled trucks and milled among the trees. Jenny put an arm around Jordy and gave him a hug.

"I figure your grandfather's got poles stashed here somewhere," she said. "We brought some too. And hay. And buckets. Here's a hammer. Nails are over there."

Albert directed operations. Saws and nails appeared. Someone found a pile of freshly cut poles beside the creek. Jordy watched in amazement, then ran to help. The boundaries of the corral would be determined by the outer edge of the trees. While the youngsters peeled poles, the men began to clear brush and put up poles. In no time Jordy could see his corral taking shape.

Joe came out. He carried his ax and hammer and headed straight for Albert.

"I'm putting the gate right here," he said, and he pushed past the chief and set to work. "Jordy!" he called, "you come here and help with the gate. It's goin' to be here."

In a few hours it was done. Jordy's corral stood ready for his horse. Two of Albert's nephews had built a feed trough, and Jenny's brother had rigged a pulley system from the creek for water.

"Get your horse," Joe told Jordy. To the others he said, "Well, it's done. I don't have enough mugs to give you all coffee, so thanks."

Albert nodded and gathered up his tools. He went over to Jordy and shook his hand. "You ever need anything," he said, "you look me up. I can always be tracked down at the general store."

Jordy smiled up at him, his eyes shining. He couldn't say a thing.

"I'll be keepin' in touch," said the chief. "You take care. And keep an eye out for your grandfather." He chuckled and patted the boy's shoulder.

Later, Jordy and his grandfather leaned against the rails, watching the mare explore her new home. She was sniffing everything and at the same time, testing the strength of the fence, butting it at regular intervals with her nose.

"That horse," said Joe, "has been her own boss 'til now. She's used to runnin' where she pleases. This new life is likely gonna be hard for her to get used to. Not only she got no freedom now, she got no friends. A horse is a herd animal, likes company. Puts a load on you, boy. You're it, you're goin' to have to be her company. She don't know that yet. You understand?"

Jordy nodded. The old man stood quietly. He was pleased with his grandson. He was pleased with the horse. Things were going to be all right, he could feel it in his bones.

"Erasmus got her halter-broke. Now she's gotta get rode. The sooner you get on her and go, the better. How do you think we should start?"

Jordy had been thinking about that. "I think first she shouldn't mind me bein' around her, touchin' her, feedin' her, things like that."

Joe smiled, pleased. The boy had horse sense.

Ten

JORDY PICKED HIS FACE OUT OF THE SNOW SLOWLY. He eased his shoulders up and looked around. The rear end of his horse was leaping and bucking away from him. He lowered his head back into the snow and sighed. His back and arms ached. He was sure something must have been pulled apart inside him.

The horse was squealing and racing around the trees in the corral. He lifted himself up to watch her run. Suddenly, she headed straight for the fence. She raised her head, stretched her neck, gathered her hindquarters under her.

"No!" yelled Jordy.

She swerved and bolted along the length of fence. Jordy leaped to his feet. Joe leaned away from the gate, breathed a sigh of relief. That had been close. If she had gone over, it would have been good-bye horse. He beckoned his grandson.

"Maybe she's not ready for the saddle," Joe said.

"Thought she was."

"Looks like she's not."

Jordy sighed and rubbed his right shoulder. He wondered what he'd done wrong. For the two weeks she'd been with him she had become amazingly agreeable to his presence. He'd spent every available moment with her, patting, feeding, grooming, talking, assuring her he was a friend until it seemed, she trusted him. It had been easy teaching her to accept a bit and bridle. He had thought she was ready for the saddle. He had expected her to accept it. He had set the saddle on the top of the fence and left it there all morning. She had sniffed at it a bit, and then ignored it. He had led her up to it and flapped the stirrups and cinch to get her used to its bumps and noises. Then he had tied her to a tree and tried to put it on her. Slowly, easily, he had settled it on her twitching back. That is when she had exploded, reared back and pulled, broken the halter rope and fled. Jordy had managed to grab the end of the rope as it whipped by him and she'd dragged him, bouncing and flailing like a tin can on the end of a car bumper, halfway around the corral.

Now she stood at the far end of the grove of trees, her nostrils flared, her ears alert, her eyes bright with surprise and indignation. Jordy walked slowly towards her, calling in his friendliest voice, "Hey girl, easy now, come on, come on, eeeasy." She danced away from his approach. He stopped, dismayed.

"Don't leave," called Joe. "Stay until she comes up to you. You gotta end the session still friends."

Jordy squatted on his haunches, small and still. Shortly, she turned in his direction and slowly came towards him.

"There girl," he crooned, "that's a girl, hey, hey."

He held out his fingers and wiggled them under her nose. She nickered. She bumped his shoulder with her head, then moved away and munched some hay at her trough. Jordy left. He felt stiff and raw. He turned to his grandfather.

"Now what do I do?"

"I don't know," said Joe. "I rode broncs. I don't know much about teachin' horses. You'd best ask Erasmus."

"I don't know where he lives."

The old man looked at the boy. Jordy looked at him. Suddenly, they both broke into laughter.

"Bull!" said Joe. "You found it in the dark."

Jordy stopped laughing. Wherever Erasmus lived it was a long way away. And he needed help with this horse.

"Maybe I'll look up Albert Greenshoots," he said.

Joe grunted.

On Sunday morning Jordy set out for the general store.

The January winds slipped and sliced along the furrows and dips and stretches of his path. He took deep breaths, feeling free. Both earth and sky were so big, sparkling, and shimmering he felt he could do anything out here. Nothing could beat him.

When he arrived at the general store, he saw its door ajar and, inside, a group of ruddy, sweating men lounging around an old stove. Albert was perched on the counter. A bottle was being passed among them. Soft laughter rippled out from their midst. They all turned as Jordy stepped towards them.

"Jordy!" Albert beamed. "Nice to see you. Everyone, this is Jordy Threebears."

Greetings swept around him, putting him at ease. "This here's the annual meetin' of the Ash Creek Cattlemen's Association," said Albert.

The men chuckled as they nodded and beckoned the boy to sit down. They were discussing the irrigation system they had set up the previous year, and they soon forgot Jordy. After a time he fell asleep in a corner surrounded by quilts and soft murmurs.

When he woke up, the store was quiet except for the muffled pops and sputters coming from the woodstove. Suddenly, there was a snort and a snore from behind the varnished oak counter. Jordy got up and tiptoed to the counter.

Albert was propped against the counter's inside shelves, his heavy head nodding over his paunch, a Hudson's Bay blanket lying haphazardly across his lap. He didn't look much like a chief. It occurred to Jordy that probably nobody did when asleep. He sat down beside Albert and watched him sleep until he stirred. Jordy coughed and Albert woke up.

"Oh, hello," yawned Albert.

"Hello."

"You been waitin' long?"

"Nope."

Albert eased himself up and put the blanket around his

shoulders. He closed his eyes and sighed. "I was dreamin' about my grandfather," he said.

"Yeah?"

"My grandfather was real old when I was little. But I remember him good." Albert opened his eyes and looked directly at Jordy as if he were looking at himself. "He used to tell me stories. It was his way of teachin'." Albert looked past the hammers and hinges arrayed behind the counter, through the frosty window, out and beyond to another time. "My grandfather's name was Albert Blackplume." Albert closed his eyes again and whispered, as if a terrible burden, a secret too hard to speak out, were being given to Jordy. "His father knew Crowfoot." Albert leaned back against the shelves, his face a mix of pride and sorrow.

"Who was Crowfoot?"

"Crowfoot," intoned Albert seriously, "was a chief. Our greatest chief."

"Oh."

"You know what he said?"

"No."

" 'Life. . . . It is the flash of a firefly in the night. . . . It is the breath of a buffalo in the wintertime. . . . It is the little shadow which runs across the grass and loses itself in the sunset.' You know what that means?"

Jordy shook his head.

"You will someday. You remember it. It's a famous thing he said. It's written on the wall in our meetin' hall."

Jordy nodded. Before he could tell Albert why he had come to see him, the chief continued, "My grandfather used to tell us stories. . . . You listenin'?"

"Yeah."

"Once," he said, "this gang of rowdies was itchin' to go raid the Crows—young guys you understand, and restless to be warriors and impress the girls. The elders said, 'Don't go; it's the wrong time of year to be botherin' the neighbors. Wait awhile.' But they couldn't wait, they were goin' right now. The elders got together and asked Spotted Tail to keep an eye on them, keep them out of trouble on account of the band bein' a little short on men at that time and not in any position to have anyone mad at them. Anyway, these young guys sneaked out of camp one night, goin' lookin' for Crows. Spotted Tail trailed them three nights, three days into Crow country. . . . They got into a mess of trouble. The Crow warriors outnumbered them four to one and had them on the run when Spotted Tail intercepted them. He came swoopin' down off a hill and placed himself between the Crows and the young Blackfoot. He was screechin' and hollerin', singin' his death song, yellin' insults at the Crows and wavin' his shield and lance at them in a rude way. They stopped up short and stared at him. He whirled around a bit and carried on and then he charged them."

"He did?"

"Yeah, he did. You see he was sacrificin' himself, givin' those other dummies a chance to get away. He put up quite a fight, too, but of course the Crows killed him. They were so impressed with him that they cut out his heart."

"They did?"

"They admired his courage."

"Oh."

"Those young guys were in big trouble when they got home, but they learned somethin'. The first thing for a warrior is the safety of his people. Glory for himself is only a bonus after what he loves is protected. . . . That was one story."

"Oh. . . . Albert? I need help with my horse. I can't get the saddle on her. Can you help me?"

"Sure. Teachin' horses anything requires that you understand how their brains work, and a few tricks, and a little patience, that's all. You'll get the hang of it quick enough. . . . You know how those little Indian ponies down south in the states could outrun the cavalry horses time after time?"

"How?"

"Well, of course, for one thing they were tough as nails. But besides that, the Indians latched onto a secret."

"Yeah?"

"Breathin'."

"Yeah?"

"They rode close to their animals, either no saddle at all or a thin one that kept them awful close to the horses' ribs. So they could feel them breathin', and they'd keep their ponies movin' in time to their breathin' rhythm. . . . And that way those ponies could keep up quite a pace a lot longer than those lumbering big soldier horses that were made to charge and then rein up half the time."

Jordy settled down beside the chief. Albert's stories fascinated him and he forgot for a moment about his problems with his horse.

"My grandfather Blackplume remembered growin' up on the prairie when all of it still belonged to us. He took me out on the plains one time and showed me the places our people used to go, and he told me the places where you used to find buffalo chips, quail, turnips, onions, berries, deer. . . ." He sighed. "Most of it ain't there now." His voice trailed off and he stared out the window. "I'm glad I knew him," he said softly. He got to his feet. "I'll drive you home," he said.

It was late afternoon by this time and already dark. Outside, the cold was piercing. Albert crossed the street to his house and yelled something in the door. They hurried into his truck and as it pulled away from the street, Albert seemed to shift mental gears and he told a happy story.

It was the story of Horst Kholer, a little boy who had been adopted by the northern Blackfoot a hundred years earlier. The Indians thought the boy was calling himself Colored Horse, so of course that's what they named him. They raised him as one of themselves and he was happy. Then an aunt tracked him down and took him to live with her in Regina. Everyone thought the boy would have a rough time back with the white people, but that wasn't how it turned out. He became just as comfortable with white people as he'd been with the Blackfoot. Still, he kept close ties to the Indians who'd raised him, and when the

Blackfoot made him an honorary chief many years later, they renamed him Two-Colors-Horse, meaning he was both red and white, but one horse all the same, a link between two peoples.

Albert drove as near as he could to Jordy's place and let him out. They felt like they were friends. Albert smiled, feeling pleased.

Jordy walked over the hill to his home, his head filled with new thoughts. He imagined his swift, bronze ancestors speeding across the plains on their fierce little ponies. He imagined himself at the head of a war party, urging his grey mare forward with a slight nudge of his knees. Maybe she could become an Indian pony! The world was suddenly charged with possibilities he'd never dreamed of before.

Eleven

ALBERT ROLLED OVER THE HILL in his 1977 pickup Saturday afternoon. He ambled up to Joe and offered him a sack of Quaker Oats. Albert barely seemed to notice Jordy, or his horse. He leaned against the side of the woodshed while Joe swung his blade, chopping firewood. The whack-thud of the chunks of cottonwood as they split and fell reverberated through the chilly air. Albert was in no hurry. Jordy waited in the corral until impatience finally overcame him and he approached the two men.

"My horse is ready," Jordy said.

"Yeah," replied Albert. He didn't move. Jordy shifted off one foot onto the other. Finally the old man was finished splitting wood and Albert stood up straight and said, "Joe, I came by to see the horse. You got time to go over her with me?"

Joe settled the ax handle more comfortably onto his shoulder. "Maybe," he said as he headed for the cabin. Jordy sighed, turned, and went back to the corral.

Eventually, first Albert, then Joe, wandered over to the corral. They leaned against the top rail, their elbows hanging over its edge, their eyes squinting into the sun-sprinkled shade, studying the mare. In less than a month she had put on weight and her thick coat shone.

"What d'you think?" asked Jordy.

Joe nodded. Albert smiled. Pride, a new sensation, bubbled up through Jordy.

"I'd like to get her saddle-broke," he said.

"What d'you think Joe?" said Albert.

"Time's right," Joe replied.

Joe brought the saddle from the cabin and Albert got a

long, heavy rope from his truck, as well as a man-sized tarpaulin. "Go ahead," said Joe, and the session began.

Albert knotted the rope onto the halter and then showed Jordy how to do a quick-release safety knot. He tied the mare to a stout tree that stood by itself near the river. The horse sensed that something unusual was happening and began to toss her head and paw the ground. Jordy stood beside her.

She reared and pulled back, expecting the rope to break and set her free as it had done before. It held. She lowered her body and crouched like the anchor man on a tug-of-war team and strained back. The tree held. She snorted and danced around the tree. Jordy stayed by her, talking quietly all the while. Albert waited. Finally she settled and stood while he brought the saddle to her.

With one massive hand he held her halter and turned her head towards him, putting her off balance. With the other, he swept the saddle up and onto her back. She shook, her sides trembled, and she began to hop in little up and down steps with her back legs. "Do up the girth!" Albert commanded, and Jordy secured the bumping contraption to her bouncing back. "Move away!" With one deft motion Albert released her head and undid the knot. She leaped away from him. Albert jiggled his end of the rope to distract her. She stopped, looked at Albert, turned to peer at the cause of the weight on her back, and then she exploded.

"Wheeeyah!!" Joe hollered. The horse was doing backtwisters and spinouts at the end of Albert's rope. Albert's red face quivered with the strain of holding her. Jordy did his best to fade into the trees, as unobtrusive as a chickadee in a gale. He was watching a process he didn't understand, and he could only hold his breath.

The mare plunged and kicked and twisted for five minutes. She could not get the saddle off. It wasn't hurting her. Shortly, her bucking lost its frantic edge, became more a token of annoyance than terror. Slowly she settled. Then she stopped.

She stood still at the end of the rope while Albert walked slowly up to her and patted her neck. He took an apple from a pocket and offered it to her. She took it and relaxed a little. He walked her around for awhile between the trees and along the fenceline so that she could feel the saddle move with her. Then he tied her to the tree again and went to get the tarp.

"Well," he told Jordy as he approached the mare once more, "by now she knows three things: she can't get away from the tree, she can't get away from the saddle, and none of this is goin' to hurt her if she don't fight."

He raised the tarp to her neck and stroked her with it. Then he draped it over the saddle, slid it off her back end, and fluttered it underneath her. She hopped and shook a bit but that was all she did. He raised it to her head, dropped it over her nose, and down her cheeks. He shook it loose and flapped it like a signal blanket in front of her. She huffed and snorted. But she did not fight.

"That's a good horse," Joe said.

"Sensible," said Albert.

Jordy emerged from the trees. The magic of the event was upon him. He had never imagined such a thing could happen—a terror-stricken horse transformed like this. He stroked her neck, feeling protective and proud of her.

"What now?" he said.

"Wanta ride her?"

"I don't know." He remembered the bone-wrenching power of her bucking.

"She's ready," said Albert softly.

But plainly, Jordy wasn't. He shook his head.

"Give her to me," said Joe as he swung over the fence and took the rope.

"Get her bridle," Joe ordered. Jordy got it.

When she was ready, Albert held her head while Joe eased his foot up into the stirrup. He stood suspended at her side for a moment, quietly patting the mare's rump. He got down and did the same on her other side, Up, down, up, down, six times, not yet attempting to put a leg over her back. Her eyes rolled back each time he stepped up in the stirrup and her ears flicked back and forth. She danced on the tips of her toes and tried a few bunny hops. Up, down, up, down, he bobbed at her side; then suddenly he swept into the saddle. It was so sudden it caught everyone by surprise. The mare flung her head back and spun around, a perfect pirouette. Albert and Jordy leapt out of the way and the mare took off. She bolted across the corral, heading straight for the fence. She swerved into the trees, leapt away from them, and bucked in rhythmic little backbusters across an opening by the river. Joe clung like fluid glue through all of it, one arm free and bobbing like a conductor's baton in time to her every move, his thin little braids flapping like independent wings.

Suddenly the horse stopped. She turned a puzzled head and looked at the man on her back. He sat there and clucked to her in soft, soothing tones. She took a step forward. Nothing happened. Then another step. She stopped and looked at him again. He clucked softly again and prodded her sides gently. Forward again. He pulled back with the reins. She stopped, startled to feel pressure in her mouth. Then another prod. Forward. Then stop. She was beginning to get the idea. He turned her head to one side and she followed her nose. He turned her the other way. He took her down by the river and rode her along the fence, then back to the gate. Then he got off.

Jordy stood transfixed. Never had he seen anything as wonderful as the old man riding the buck and the fear out of that horse.

"Been awhile, eh?" said Albert.

Joe nodded. He handed the reins to Jordy and went to the cabin. Albert shook his head, then he chuckled and laid an arm across Jordy's shoulders.

"Ain't always that easy, you know," he said. "Some-times the critters fight like mad for hours. Sometimes they try to kill you. Sometimes they kill themselves. Some of them are real mean. Some of 'em never learn, end up as broncs in a rodeo."

"Yeah?"

"Your horse now, she's good. She's smart. She's not likely to try anything downright rotten."

Jordy nodded.

"Doesn't mean to say she won't try you out though. She will. Horse has gotta do that. Find out who's boss. You remember that. She'll test you."

"Oh."

"Tomorrow you saddle her up again. Remember that knot?"

"Yeah."

"Good. Saddle her up every day, walk her around. When you feel like it, get on her."

When Jordy went into the cabin after Albert had gone he was startled to see his grandfather lying on his cot, his face ashen, his arms limp. The old man was staring at the ceiling as if something up there had just played a dirty trick on him.

"Joe? What's the matter?"

"I'm old, dammit," he said.

"You sure rode the horse good."

"Yeah." He turned his head away and closed his eyes.

He was remembering the easy power of his youth, the effortless ease with which he had made his way through the world. Surely it hadn't been that long ago that he'd been able to stay with some whirling bronc, crash into the dust, pick himself up, and saunter away for another crunching ride. His power, he had thought, was endless. Of course in his head he had known that seventy-year-old men do not do the work of youngsters, but in his heart he had always harbored the notion that through strength of will he could keep the effects of creeping age away. But there was no denying the terrible, overwhelming tiredness he felt.

"You want some coffee?" Jordy asked.

"Uh . . . no . . . thanks."

Joe smiled at his grandson. He was a good kid and Joe was acquiring a certain affection for him. He said, "When your mother was your age she wanted to be a ballerina. Didn't know the first thing about it except she thought it looked good. Of course, there was no damned way...." His voice trailed off. Then he looked up at the ceiling again. A faint chuckle whispered through his chest. "You ever get married Jordy, you stay home. I was away so much my wife ran off with some damned white man from Vancouver. You get a woman, you stick by her. They don't like being left behind. You understand?"

Jordy nodded.

"Another thing." He paused to catch his breath. "Bring in the firewood. It's workin' up to a storm."

"Joe? . . . Thanks for riding my horse."

"Oh, never mind that. . . . You know? Albert ain't so bad."

"Yeah."

Twelve

JORDY'S LIFE HAD BECOME AGREEABLY SIMPLE. At school he stayed out of trouble. At home he either helped his grandfather with chores, did homework, or worked with his horse. He had only one problem. He was afraid to ride his horse.

Albert gave him an all-about-riding book and he read all of it carefully. Joe told him stories about bronc riding and explained about balance and about anticipating a horse's moves. Jordy remembered every word. Still, when he saddled the mare and walked her around, as she danced beside him, her head tossing and her tail swishing, all he could think of was the wild power of her bucking.

One day after school in early February, Miss Mac-Tavish approached him after class. "Jordy," she said, "my assistant for the senior boy's basketball team quit. You've been such a help to me. Would you be interested in the job?"

"Not really—I mean, I don't have time. I'm too busy with my horse."

"You have a horse?" Her eyes brightened and she smiled.

"Yeah, only I can't ride her yet."

"Why not?"

He explained. Her smile broadened. And then she laughed.

"Listen," she said, "maybe we're both in for a run of luck." Then she explained that she gave riding lessons to a blind girl. Her student wanted a riding companion. Her goal was to enter an endurance race but she needed more lessons in a riding ring before she could consider it. Would

Jordy serve as her riding mate, provided Miss MacTavish taught him to ride?

"Uh, well, I . . ." he stammered. "What's an endurance race?"

"It's a test of horsemanship for the rider, a test of endurance and courage for the horse. Horses race a course usually of 50 or 100 miles through natural terrain. The first horse to cross the finish line, or the horse to do it in the fastest time in good condition, wins. I used to compete, but I don't have the time or the horse now. Emily, the blind girl, has had it in her head that she would like to try it, ever since she read about a blind endurance rider in the states."

Jordy's eyes were sparkling.

"Would you be interested in riding with Emily?"

He wasn't sure he liked the idea of riding with a blind girl, but he was sure he wanted this opportunity to learn to ride. With little hesitation he said, "Yeah."

On Saturday, Miss MacTavish picked up Jordy on Main Street, drove past Glendon and up to the MacKenzie ranch.

"We're here," she said as they pulled up in front of a Tudor-style mansion. "The MacKenzie's. Filthy rich." She laughed. "They own a lot of land around here."

Jordy looked around. The house was immense. Spread out behind the house were paddocks and loafing sheds, each section containing a prize animal of some sort—horse, cow, bull. Past that was pastureland rolling away into the hills. To the right of the house stood the barn and beyond that a building Jordy guessed must be either a warehouse or an arena. To the left of the house was the driveway bordered by meticulously cultivated woodlands.

MacTavish steered her car behind the barn to a parking lot taken up by neat rows of tractors, trucks, a bulldozer, backhoe, and horse trailer. Jordy's attention was rivetted to a shiny black truck. A buzz of fear prickled across his head. Miss MacTavish stopped in front of a sign: RIDING INSTRUCTOR.

"Well. This is it," she said.

They were met in the barn by the ranch foreman. He was tall, lean, and cold like a steel trap. His ice-blue eyes swept past MacTavish and stared at Jordy. His jaw was clenched and he said through thin lips, "Who's he?"

"Fred Brady, I'd like you to meet Jordy Threebears."

The foreman's ruddy cheeks had suddenly paled. The muscles on the outer edges of his eyes twitched and he drew back from them.

"What's he doin' here?" he said in a voice so low they barely heard it.

"He's come to help."

"Huh." The foreman snorted, turned, and left them, calling over his shoulder as he disappeared into a feed room, "Your horses are ready, saddled at the arena."

Miss MacTavish glanced at Jordy. His eyes were bright and hard and he was staring at the feed room door, a stare full of fear and loathing like she had never seen before.

"Jordy, ah, I'm sorry.... I don't know what's gotten into him today," she said.

He turned and looked at her. He shook his head. "Forget it," he whispered.

They walked through the barn, past rows of horses in spacious box stalls and on through the bright February sun to the arena. The smells of sawdust and horses greeted them as the door slid open and they stood at the end of the training ring. At one side, two horses stood tied and a girl sat on a bench waiting.

Miss MacTavish introduced Jordy to Emily. Jordy felt awkward. He didn't know where to look or what to do. One quick glance at Emily, with her head tilted up and off to one side as her blind eyes flicked and rolled, unnerved him. "Hi," he mumbled to his shoes. He turned to Miss MacTavish, waiting for instructions. "What do I do?" he said.

"Stand here for now with me while I put Emily through her paces. She and the horse will be going around us in a circle. It's called 'longeing'. Watch."

The teacher boosted the girl into a flat little saddle, gave her the reins, walked her out to the middle of the ring and said, "Take the left rein." Emily moved her horse off to the left, and to Jordy's surprise, a long line held by Miss MacTavish unravelled from the horse's head.

Horse and rider moved in a circle around Miss MacTavish and Jordy. The teacher called out instructions and Emily shifted accordingly. "Sit deeper, lower your hands, heels down. That's good! Relax your neck."

It was a revelation to Jordy. He had supposed you just jumped on the horse's back, clucked, and took off.

Except for the unnerving deadness of her eyes, Emily was pretty. Jordy had not failed to notice. He liked the set of her chin as she settled into the position the teacher was looking for. Her long legs and back seemed to flow with the horse's stride. The brown braid down her back swung softly in time to the horse's rhythm. The sense he'd had of Emily being incomplete was gone.

"Prepare to trot—and—trrrot!"

Horse and rider moved together into a crisp, pounding trot. Around and around they went, then back to a walk, then a canter, and finally back again to a walk. Emily moved with the horse in graceful harmony, her cheeks now rosy, head straight, manner composed. She seemed fit to challenge the world when she sat on a horse. They stopped for a moment, then repeated the whole process in the other direction.

Jordy stood breathless in the center, watching every move and shift of pace. The girl had guts, he thought. It was beautiful—the girl, the horse, the precision and control. Suddenly he had a whole new idea of what riding could be. Miss MacTavish unhooked Emily's horse from the longe line and set Jordy on the other horse.

He could see the top of Miss MacTavish's head. He could feel the horse breathing beneath him. The world looked different. The horse shifted its weight. He reached forward and patted its neck. He could smell its warm, oaty sweat. He felt good.

"That was longeing, Jordy," MacTavish said. "I'd like to do that with you next lesson. For today, I think it would be best if you just relax on a horse, get the feel of it. . . . Go down to the other end of the arena with Emily, walk around a bit, stay together."

She explained how to steer the horse, get it to stop or speed up. Jordy took a deep breath and gathered up the reins. He gave the horse a timid nudge and turned its head. To his delight the horse walked where he had aimed it and ambled across the sawdust ring beside Emily's mount.

"If you talk to me I can follow your voice," Emily said.

"Huh?"

"I'll follow you. . . . Make a trail of sound and see if I can follow it."

It was embarrassing at first to hum and cluck and whistle while he steered his mount around the ring, back and forth making a pattern of sound. But when she found him and laughed, he forgot about himself and became engrossed in the game. He set off on another pattern and she found him again. He stared at her eyes. They looked as if they had been blue once but had been smeared with a chalky thumbprint. Now they were an indistinct smudge in slightly sunken caverns.

"Don't stare," she said.

He was startled. How could she know he was staring? He felt unsure of what to do or where to look. The tilt of her chin was defiant, demanding respect, daring him to think of any reason not to give it. He turned away from her, headed towards the other end and called to her.

"Come find me."

They played this game for an hour. It became so absorbing that they forgot about the teacher, about everything but the puzzles of sound and motion he wove all over the rectangle of sawdust they rode on. And he realized, by the time they'd finished, that he was sitting on his horse effortlessly, well balanced, at perfect ease.

Apart from the brief, disturbing encounter with the

foreman, Jordy was delighted with the afternoon. He was thrilled finally to be up on a horse. And he liked Emily. Only the foreman and the memory of the black truck that had run him off the road tinged his happiness with apprehension. He was sure Fred Brady had been the driver that day.

A week later, after the second session at the ranch, Jordy saddled his own horse, determined to ride. He walked her around the corral, eyeing her nervously. But she ambled along beside him, used, by now, to these little walks with a saddle on her back.

He stopped her in the thickest part of the grove of trees and quietly patted her neck for a long time. When he felt courage firmly inside him, he moved slowly to her side and put a foot up in the stirrup. He took a deep breath and swept into the saddle. She tried to duck out from under him, to whirl, but she had no room to maneuver and so she stood and shook.

"Hey, hey, easy girl, easy does it." He was shaking too. His heart was racing. "Easy, easy," he told himself. He sat still and loose, asking nothing, wanting only stillness from her. Eventually the horse quietened. Gently he nudged her forward. She responded. His heart filled with joy.

He got on and off several times, each time more slowly than the time before. She accepted this. He knew they'd begun a partnership. He knew he was going to be a rider.

Thirteen

"JORDY THREEBEARS," SAID MS. SAMPSON through her thin, arched nose, "you haven't done your homework, *again!* Do you want to fail grade nine?"

Jordy stared at her and said nothing.

"Young man, I expect you to answer me when I talk to you."

"What?"

"Why haven't you got your homework done?"

"I don't have time."

"You'd better make time young man, or you'll be spending another year in grade nine."

He stared at the worksheet on his desk. Adverbial clauses. Jordy had more important things on his mind. All he could think of was Sunday. On Sunday he was going to ride his horse out on the prairie. His heartbeat quickened at the thought.

He had been progressing well in his riding lessons and he felt confident that he could handle a horse at any gait. He had been riding every day but always inside the corral. The mare accepted his weight on her back and responded to his direction. Jordy was sure he was ready to put her training to the test.

"Jordy! GET TO WORK!"

Jordy sighed. School was such a pain. He fiddled with his pen and bent over his work. I'll bet Joe never bothered with junk like this, he thought.

"You not been doin' your work," said Joe that night as his fingers tightened over the note from school.

"It's dumb, Joe. Why should I have to know that stuff?"

Joe sat down at his workbench and closed his eyes. His hands moved lightly over the pieces of leather and fur strewn across the tabletop. He loved his work, the feel and smell of leather, the shapes he cut out, the rattles, pouches, miniature tipis, drums, bows, and arrows he created. And yet he didn't want Jordy making such things for a living thirty years from now.

"I'll tell ya somethin', boy. . . ." Joe's voice was low and an unfamiliar intensity vibrated in it. Jordy sat down.

"I met a lotta Indians in prison. Most of 'em couldn't even read or write. They didn't know nothin' about nothin'. Some of 'em didn't even know why they were in jail. You wanta grow up stupid? You need book learnin' if you wanta get along."

"Huh." Jordy was sure that whatever happened to him, he wasn't going to be stupid, but his grandfather's insistence on book learning surprised him.

The next day, Emily greeted Jordy in a miserable mood similar to his own. After the lesson, when they were unsaddling their horses, she came and tugged his sleeve.

"Jordy," she asked softly, "do you know Fred Brady from somewhere else?"

"Why?"

"He told Daddy he shouldn't let me ride with you and Daddy's starting to backpeddle about letting us ride out on the prairie together."

"That's dumb." As he said this the muscles in Jordy's face tightened and he threw the saddle down with surprising force.

"I don't understand it. Fred really has it in for you."

Jordy couldn't say a thing. The memory of the black truck coming at him made his knees weak and his fists shake. At last he looked at Emily and said, "Brady ever messes with me again, I'll kill him."

"What?"

"He ran me off the road once. I don't know why, unless he just loves to try and kill people who walk by themselves."

"Gee." She was quiet as she brushed off her horse. Then she said, "Well, he's not going to spoil our plans to ride out on the prairie. I'll speak to Daddy."

"I'm goin' to ride my horse outside the corral tomorrow, get her used to riding in the open, and along roads. We'll go for that ride. . . ."

Sunday dawned clear and warm. Spring's first gentle touch was tickling the wind. A strong, steady energy was pulsing up from the awakening earth, filtering into the slow, winter blood of the horse. Jordy felt it too. He looked around, took a deep breath. Today was the day! Sunshine sparkled on the snowy rocks beside Ash Creek and enveloped the still-dormant trees. It sprinkled tiny points of light over the little mare's coat.

Jordy put her halter on and brushed her briskly. She bobbed her head and stomped her feet, keen with health and spirit. He saddled and bridled her, then went to the gate and swung it open. He took her to the farthest corner of the corral and there he mounted. Calmly he walked her around the trees and along the fenceline, his every muscle relaxed, telling her there was nothing to worry about, until they came to the opening. She stopped, startled to see the barrier gone.

She lifted her head, flicked her nostrils in and out, testing the wind. He urged her forward and she danced through the gate, suddenly unsure and spooky. He steered her to the cabin and she snorted and sniffed at it as if it had never been there before. He let her explore the outhouse, the woodshed, the back of the cabin, the tire tracks, whatever caught her curiosity. She danced around all of it. Then he turned her and headed out onto the open prairie.

The horse moved with grace and there was spring and power in her muscles. Jordy lifted his head and let out a whoop of joy and the little grey mare broke into a happy, staccato trot that lengthened and quickened as they left the cabin and corral behind. She was covering ground with big, bold strides that forced Jordy to adjust his grip and struggle for balance. He eased himself back and tried to station his bouncing behind firmly on the saddle. For a moment he sat into it and felt an instant sensation of security and balance. He was moving with his horse. Then he lost it, his backside was flung out of its nest, and he was all askew again.

The horse solved the problem. She let go of the trot and shifted into a run, a stretched out, flat down, all out run.

Jordy sucked in air and clung to her back, as still as a blade of grass in the eye of a hurricane, while the steady, straight-line rhythm of the animal beneath him rocketed them over the earth.

She ran and ran, always keeping to the winding course of the creek. The intensity of her stride began to ease, until a sense of rhythm came to Jordy and he moved his body forward, crouching close to her flying mane, pumping his arms in time to the beat of her stride. In that instant they ceased being rider and horse and became almost as one creature, flowing together as they raced on.

Ahead Jordy could see the faint outline of a fence, a good place to bring the run down to a walk. He was sure the mare would object and he readied himself. He sat up straight, deepened his back, and took control of the reins.

"Slooow," he said in deep, soft tones. "Sloow, girl."

She struggled to keep running. "Whoa!" he said in his deepest voice. Authority rang in it.

She stopped, danced up and down on her toes and shook her head, banging her teeth together in agitation. He shifted in the saddle, released some slack into the reins, and urged her forward. She stepped ahead.

Jordy walked her a mile down the fenceline until they came to a gate. He got off and opened it, and on they went. The horse broke into a quiet jog, and Jordy hummed a little chant, hey-hey-yeh, in time to her stride as they travelled over the pasturelands and fields of the reserve. After awhile, he headed for home.

By the time they reached Main Street, both of them

were tired. Jordy's legs and back ached. The horse's head hung low. As they passed the schoolyard, Jordy barely noticed the approach of a tall, thin woman until she called.

"Hello, young man."

He stopped his horse. "Hello," he said.

"My goodness, dear, the two of you look to be on your last legs."

He nodded and reached down to pat the animal's sweaty neck. "It's been a long day," he said.

"You must have come quite a distance."

"Yeah. It's her first ride. Mine too, out in the open."

"Would you like to stop and rest for a minute? I live behind the school and I could make you a cup of hot chocolate."

"Yeah?" He eyed her carefully.

"My name is Marabel Hind," she said. "I'm the teacher here."

"Yeah?"

"Yes. Who, may I ask, are you?"

"Jordy Threebears."

"I thought so." She smiled at him. "I taught your mother. Wonderful girl, Sarah was."

He got off the horse and waited by her porch while she hurried into the house to fix a drink for him. The chocolate was hot and steamy and as he sipped it she talked about horses and cattle. He was surprised that this lace-and-flower-teacup lady knew so much about ranching.

"You taught my mother?" he asked in a pause.

"Yes. She was a diligent student."

"You taught me?"

"Well, no. The year you were in grade one, I had a year's leave of absence, and your grade-two year had barely begun when your mother was killed and you were gone."

He felt uneasy, as if he was in the presence of facts he could know if he reached for them. But he was tired and let the opportunity slide by.

He studied his hands briefly and sighed. "Do you think a horse needs a name?" he asked.

"Oh, I suppose it's helpful to have something to call it. Does your horse have a name?"

"No. I haven't found a name yet, not one that seems right. . . ."

"I'm sure you'll find the right name."

"It's gotta be a name that comes from her. . . ." He sighed again, unsure exactly why a name mattered, and why it was eluding him.

"Have you had your horse long?" she asked.

Jordy told her about the mare and what he'd learned thus far. She listened to every word and then she said, "Just consider one thing, Jordy. Suppose I was going to teach you the violin. It would be unwise of me to make your first real lesson six hours long."

"So?"

"Well, dear, you have made this little horse's first real ride six hours long."

"Oh." He groaned inwardly. She was right. What had he been thinking of? He looked at the mare. Her ears had fallen over, one hip was down, her back was hunched. She was in his care and already he had hurt her.

"What should I do?"

"Well, dear, I wouldn't ride her home. I'd walk beside her. I'd be extra careful looking after her when you get home. Keep her warm, watch for colic, brush and massage her. And I wouldn't ride like that again until she's ready. You need to build up a horse's tolerance for training and work gradually."

When Jordy reached home he was cold and stiff. The mare, on the other hand, was beginning to recover. The weightless walk had done her good. Nonetheless, Jordy brushed her and blanketed her, made a warm bran mash, and piled extra hay in her manger. Then he went into the cabin, straight to his room, and collapsed on the bed.

Joe shuffled to his door and peered in. "You want a cup of coffee?"

"No . . . thanks." Jordy looked at his grandfather. He felt very small and stupid. He said, "Joe, I didn't think I could be this tired."

"That's okay, happens to all of us." Joe smiled.

"Yeah."

"You have a good ride?"

"Yeah."

"You learn anything?"

"Uh huh."

"Good."

Fourteen

A WARM, LAZY WIND FLUTTERED through the prairie grasses and shook the new leaves of the cottonwoods. The early May sun shone in streamers of light through the trees and sparkled over the prairie. Jordy could hear Emily laugh from across the meadow. He clucked softly to the mare and she picked up her head and swung into an easy jog. He stopped his horse where Emily stood by her horse and got off.

"Well," he said.

"Well?" she laughed again, with sunlight and shade like a quilt covering her.

"We can continue."

"Then let's go!" She was impatient. She mounted her horse and waited for Jordy to lead the way.

He moved the horses out in a light jog. They travelled across the meadow and over a rise, and as they went he hummed his little chant, hey-hey-yeh-hey, in time to the trot-trot of the horses' stride.

This was their first outing and Emily could feel a current of joy rush through her. She called, "Hey, Jordy, can't we go any faster?" and was pleased to hear the increased tempo of his horse in answer. The sensation of free, swinging speed was euphoric. She wanted to go on like this forever.

Jordy felt that same surge of happiness. Finally, he was free, master of himself and his horse, racing over the prairie. He felt he could go anywhere, do anything.

The mare stretched herself, eager to run. She was in superb condition. The more Jordy rode her, the stronger she got. She covered the twenty miles to the MacKenzie ranch with a long, swinging stride, an easy floating motion that Jordy had finally learned to sit to.

Jordy headed towards a pond nestled in a dip in the prairie. It was here he wanted to stop for their picnic. His eyes scanned everything on the way. It was up to him to see that the path was clear of danger and he took this responsibility very seriously. He had spent more than one wakeful night worrying about the possibility of an accident, and he was alert and wary, now that they were riding in the open.

They dismounted by the pond and settled down for lunch. The sky was clear and bright, a pure sweep of blue. They leaned back on their elbows, and while Emily lifted her face to take in the full touch of the sun, Jordy took the sandwiches he had made from the saddlebag by his arm.

"Gee, I feel good," she said. "I bet we could go clear across Canada."

"Huh."

"What d'you mean, 'huh'?"

"We could with my horse, but not yours. Chuck is too slow."

"He's just right."

"For followin' along he is, but not for hard goin'!"

He passed her a sandwich and they ate. Afterwards, Emily hummed a little tune. He cocked his head.

"Sounds nice."

"Beethoven."

"What's that?"

"Beethoven was a person. He made music. I love his stuff. He couldn't even hear. He couldn't hear what you just heard."

"Yeah?"

"Imagine being a composer, loving music more than anything, and not being able to hear it. He wanted to kill himself."

"Yeah?"

"But he didn't. He was a fighter, and he beat deafness."

In strong, rich tones she whistled a joyful song that

triggered the happy feeling Jordy had when he was trotting his horse across open country. He grinned.

"You're a pretty good whistler."

"That's my favorite. *Ode to Joy.* A song for winners. I'll play it for you when we get home if you like."

"Naw. I think I'll head back to my place real quick."

"Oh . . . yeah. I suppose everyone will be mad when we get back."

"Yeah."

"Well, I don't care. It's about time they started letting me live my life my own way."

Their happy mood vanished. The foreman's threatening presence hung between them. Whatever he had said to Jacob MacKenzie had cast doubt about Jordy on Jacob's mind. He had told Emily again that he didn't want her alone with Jordy.

"I'm glad we came anyway," she said defiantly, "no matter what they think or say."

"I'm takin' good care of you," he said softly.

"But I know they'll have a fit when they find out we snuck off."

When they arrived back at the ranch they were greeted by a barrage of angry questions. Like two over-heated howitzers, Emily's parents fired questions without waiting for answers. Was Emily all right? Where had they gone? What had they been doing? Why hadn't they checked with someone before they'd left?

"When will you get off my back?" Emily yelled. "I'm sixteen years old and if I want to go out for awhile I will! I won't spend my entire life asking for permission every time I want to breathe."

"There's no need to be rude," said Emily's mother.

"I'm not a helpless baby!"

"Emily!" her father bellowed. "If this is how you're going to act, we'll just forget your riding. If you can't talk decently to your mother, if this is where your riding leads you, I won't have it. You can take needlepoint until you remember some manners."

"No!"

"Yes!"

"You can't do that!"

"I won't have you two running off into the hills whenever you please!"

"I got her home safe."

Jacob paused to regard Jordy. What he'd heard from Fred Brady and what he'd heard from Emily and Miss MacTavish were so different, he didn't know what to think about this boy.

"I see that," he said. "But I will not have my daughter taking off like that. I won't stand for it. Do you understand?"

"Uh huh. . . ."

"Oh, Daddy, we were okay. We were very careful, I was so happy."

"We'll talk about this later." Mrs. MacKenzie had calmed down a little. "Jordy, please put the horses away. Emily, come to the house."

Jordy took Chuck to the barn. He walked him down the alleyway to the tack room, tied him up, and unsaddled him. He worked quietly, aware of the warm smells of leather, sawdust, and horse all around him, thinking about the happiness of their day and how it had been spoiled. He wondered what the foreman could have said to Mr. MacKenzie.

Suddenly, a dark form emerged from the shadows. Fred Brady came towards him, his eyes fixed intently on Jordy's face.

"So how was it?" he drawled.

"How was what?"

"Aw come on. You creeps don't fool me. . . . How was it?"

"What?"

Brady leaned against the stall door, casually fingering a blade of hay. Jordy tensed. He looked around quickly, checking out escape routes. His heart was pounding. Neither of them noticed Jacob's approach.

"You think yer gettin' on good with the old man's daughter, don't ya? Gettin' yerself into a cozy little situation.... You Indians are all alike, just itchin' for some white girl.... What'd ya do in the bush, ya little bastard?"

Fred moved away from the stall and slowly walked towards Jordy, his chin thrust out, his eyes ice-cold. Jordy backed away. Slowly, Fred flicked the bit of hay away from his fingers, drew them together into a fist.

"Yer mother was a dog," he said.

Rage exploded in Jordy and he catapulted himself head first into the man's guts. Instantly arms like steel girders wrapped around the boy, squeezing the life out of him. Jordy drove one knee upward with all the force of his rage. Fred gasped and staggered backwards into the arms of Jacob MacKenzie.

"Hey!" MacKenzie bellowed. He flung the folding body away from him. "What's going on around here? What's it all about, Jordy?" Jordy could say nothing. He was seething with confusion and anger. Jacob turned to the foreman. "Fred?" The foreman was still gasping for air. "I won't have this!" Jacob bellowed. "I demand an explanation. Jordy, what happened?"

Jordy looked from MacKenzie to the foreman, his heart pounding wildly.

"Can't you talk?"

"He said ... he ... I ..." Jordy stammered.

"I heard what he said."

"So I rammed him.... He called my mother a dog!"

"I heard him."

"I hate him! I'll kill him!" Jordy lunged toward the prostrate foreman.

"No you won't." Jacob grabbed him firmly. "Settle down, son," he said, and when Jordy had finally stopped quivering, Jacob released him and stood back. "I'm sorry this happened, Jordy. You had better take your horse and leave now. If you want to ride with Emily next week, you're welcome."

Jordy stared at MacKenzie, then without a word wheeled and ran.

After the boy had gone, MacKenzie walked over to the foreman, bent down, and said, "Fred, you're fired."

When Jordy got home Joe could see immediately that something bad had happened. He made his grandson a cup of coffee and then he asked, "What's wrong?"

"I got into a fight."

"Yeah? With who?"

"The foreman—Fred Brady."

"What about?"

"He called my mother a dog." Even now, Jordy's voice shook.

"Did you get him?"

"Yeah."

"Good."

Joe turned to making supper. As he stirred the stew, memories he'd tried so hard to bury barrelled into his head. As clear as prairie air, they were still vivid. The news, Sarah was dead, the consuming rage, all the colors and textures of feeling belonging to that point in time, welled up again inside him. Even now, eight years later, the hurt was so bad he trembled as he thought of what they'd done. His beautiful daughter. Yes, he would kill every last one of them right now if he could.

"Joe? You all right?" Anxiously Jordy touched Joe's sleeve.

Joe opened his eyes. He turned and saw his grandson, the living image of his daughter. At the sight of the boy, the thoughts of revenge and grief evaporated. In that moment he knew he would never again give in to that brand of justice. There was the boy to consider.

"I'm okay," he said.

They were quiet while they ate supper. A sense of menace hung in the air. The past was not out of the way yet. It seemed its influence still slipped between the threads they tried to weave.

Later, Joe lay in his bed feeling the kind of tension he

remembered feeling in his cell before a prison riot. The air was thick with it. He rolled onto his back and lifted his head, listening, his nerves on edge. He sat up, restless. Something was wrong but he could not define it.

Jordy felt it, too. He could not sleep. Finally, he got out of bed, dressed, and tiptoed to the outer room to get his boots.

"Jordy?" Joe whispered, "somethin' wrong?"

"I don't feel good. Goin' to check my horse."

Together they went outside. A million stars gave aid to the two as their eyes searched the corral. The bright, fat moon beamed its silver light through the rustling trees, but could not show them what they wanted to see. The mare had vanished.

Fifteen

JORDY AND JOE SPENT THE NIGHT rumbling over the reserve in the old man's truck, searching the roadsides for hoofprints in the moonlight. They checked fencelines and gates. They woke up half their neighbors but no one had heard or seen anything. There was no sign of the little horse anywhere. Jordy began to fear she'd been stolen and his suspicions turned to Fred Brady. By morning he was frantic.

"She's gotta be around here somewhere!" he cried. "She's gotta be!" He slammed his fists into the dashboard of the truck.

"Maybe she's run to the MacKenzie's. She knows the way," Joe said.

"Yeah, maybe." A small spark of hope lit the interior of his dismal heart.

But the MacKenzies hadn't seen the horse. Nor did anyone spot her after a day of searching. Jordy and Joe returned home that night in silence, suspicion and sorrow settling in their separate minds and hearts.

"It's not fair," Jordy whispered to the old man as they sipped their coffee in the cabin that night.

"Huh," Joe snorted, "you mess with whitemen, you get burned. Things always end bad." He sighed once and turned to his worktable where he clipped and stitched his tourist trinkets in numb and sullen silence.

"I'm goin' to check with Erasmus," Jordy said. "He can find her—he's got to." His voice shook and his eyes were bright with tears. However things ended for his grandfather, he could not bear that it should be that way for him.

The next day Jordy borrowed a mount from Jacob MacKenzie and rode out to Erasmus's cabin. They searched through the hills and plains for days. The mare was not running the range with the wild horses. She was not in anyone's pasture or barn. She was nowhere.

He sat in the flickering light of their campfire on their last night of searching and shivered in the chill night air. A feeling of terrible gloom and hurt gripped him with its dark arms.

"Joe thinks it's no use," he whispered.

"Nuthin's no use."

"Joe thinks everything ends bad."

"Huh. She's gotta be somewhere. She'll turn up."

Jordy looked at Erasmus's large, craggy face as the firelight touched it. The big man seemed so calm and sure. Jordy broke a blade of grass and stuck it between his teeth.

"Erasmus?" he said, "how come Joe doesn't like white folks?"

"Well now . . ." Erasmus paused. "Every man's got his own particular reasons for the way he thinks. Your grandfather's been hit with some low blows."

"What about you?"

"Me?" Erasmus chuckled softly to himself, then his brow furrowed and his eyes darkened. "I'll tell ya somethin' kid. Joe got reason to see things the way he does, but me? I'll tell ya, don't matter a man's white or Indian, not to me."

"Why not?"

"Because it's all the same, red man, white man. I'll tell ya somethin'. Indians can be just as dumb and disgustin' as whites. I leave 'em all alone."

"Why?"

Erasmus was quiet a long time. His eyes drifted over the peaceful prairie. He poked the embers at the edge of the fire and then he said, "My daddy was a drunk. He smacked us around all the time. My sister married a white guy, anything to get away, and you know what?"

"What."

"When she was with whites she was Harry's squaw, just an Indian, and when she was with Indians she had no status, she was as good as white, and her children were nuthin'." The lines in his face twitched and his fists closed. "Some reserves, yours for instance, doin' okay. Mine had some real losers, whiners, drunks, everyone makin' excuses. Nobody can convince me any people's better or worse than another on the strength of their color."

"Yeah?"

"You wanta be an Indian? Be an Indian. Nuthin' can stop you. You wanta be a good man? Be a good man. Wanta be a bum? Be a bum. It's up to you. You wanta find your horse, you keep at it until you do. Make up your mind nuthin's gonna stop you. You'll find her."

Jordy returned home the next day, subdued and watchful. Everywhere he went, he looked for her. Every morning, as soon as he was up, he checked the corral, in the hope that she had come home, despite the deepening fear that she had been stolen.

He returned to school. He did his homework but only because life was so empty now and there was nothing else to do. He stayed up late doing it, hoping to wear himself out so he could sleep. But sleep was no consolation, nor did it come easily, no matter how tired he made himself. Nightmares plagued him.

The most persistent dream was of the mare. . . . She was stepping lightly over the moon-flecked prairie, coming towards him, her head bobbing softly in time to her steps. He rose out of the slightly waving grasses, extending his hands to her. "Come," he sang in a single note that filled the air like crystal light. She stopped, raised her head, and saw him. She swung into a free, happy trot, one so smooth she seemed to float towards him. Then a black truck appeared, roaring out of the wind to descend between them. The horse skidded to a stop and reared. A dozen black man-shapes scrambled out of the truck and ran towards her with fists and beer bottles flying. She turned and raced away while Jordy screamed into the sky, "No! No!" The shapes pivoted and came at him instead. . . .

He turned to Emily for comfort. He felt at home with her. On the reserve, he still felt out of place even though he was getting to know some of the kids who had visited him in the hospital. Sometimes it surprised him to realize he was a Blackfoot, among his own people. He felt more like an exile from somewhere he couldn't remember very well, living in a new country he didn't understand yet. But with Emily he was comfortable. Her parents apparently had decided that Jordy was okay. Mr. MacKenzie let him have the run of the ranch and ride any horse he chose. Mrs. MacKenzie invited him to the house after their lessons and fed him cocoa and muffins.

One day, as Emily and Jordy were saddling their horses, she suddenly stopped and turned to him. "Jordy?" she said timidly, "may I touch you?" Before he could answer she came close to him and put her fingers on his face. Gently, methodically, her hands ranged over his forehead, eyes, nose, cheeks, mouth, chin, and neck. She held his head between her hands and quietly stroked his hair. Satisfied, she stepped back and declared, "Jordy, I think you're handsome."

"Yeah?" he said, pleased.

"Yes. Jordy, when are you going to learn the word 'yes', Y-E-S?"

"Yeah."

She'd laughed and on an impulse wrapped him in a brief, warm hug.

He took Emily for another picnic ride, but it wasn't the same. He could only think how much he missed his mare, and his customary chant stuck in his throat. He was silent and sad.

"Let's go in a race," Emily said to cheer him up. "A real race, see if we can do it."

Jordy shrugged and looked away. No matter how nice anyone was to him, nothing could take away the sadness and aloneness he felt. However kind the MacKenzies, Miss

MacTavish, Mr. Campbell, or anyone else was to him, it could not change the fact that his horse was lost.

Still, he would not give up. He knew if he lost hope, he would lose everything. Erasmus had to be right.

Sixteen

WHEN MR. CAMPBELL INVITED JORDY to the June first rodeo in Harriott, Jordy immediately said yes. Rodeo had been the world of his father and he longed to be close to it.

They drove to the rodeo grounds at noon, into a carnival maze of horse trailers, pickup trucks, campers and cars, clusters of cowboys and horses, and everywhere the smell of beer, onions, leather, horse, and dirt. They parked in the lot and walked back through the grounds to the arena. Jordy soaked up everything. He heard the sounds of horses and crowds muffled in the sawdusty air. He saw the saddles on the ground, the horses like patient sentries tied at the backs of trailers, their noses methodically poking into hay nets. He watched the cowboys leaning into their trucks, sucking at beer bottles, adjusting chaps, coiling ropes. Sweat trickled through his hair and past his eyes as he and Mr. Campbell wove their way through the grounds to the grandstand and climbed to their seats in the blazing sun. A cowboy chorus of yips and whistles broke out as a bull exploded under a madly raking rider in the arena. The sound system crackled as the announcer gave the score and the name of the rider, and the crowd murmured its editorial.

Behind the arena lay the holding pens where calves and bulls and broncs milled about in subdued distress. Jordy watched as the wranglers prodded a bunch of bawling calves to the chutes.

Mr. Campbell slipped his fishing cap back off his forehead. "Next event is Little Britches Calf Riding," he said. "Must be for children."

A calf came tearing out of the chute with a little boy

clinging to its back. It whirled and bucked and bawled. The miniature cowboy jerked and flapped on its back like a fish on a line, his hand caught in the cinching. His hat flew off, his head snapped back as the calf's rear flipped up. The buzzer sounded and instantly the clown and a cowboy grabbed the baby steer and rescued its rider. The score was broadcast and the little fellow picked his hat out of the dust and sauntered to the railing with all the masculine swagger of a prize fighter.

Jordy was not watching the event in the arena. His eyes were cruising through the campgrounds, going from horse to horse.

"I never thought such little children could do this sort of thing," said Mr. Campbell. "I mean, well, they're so small, and it's dangerous, it's a wonder they don't get killed you know. . . ."

Slowly Jordy turned his gaze back to the arena as the next little rider was catapulted out of the chute. "They wouldn't do it if they didn't want to," he said.

"Oh, I suppose not. . . ."

"Everyone's gotta learn to get hurt."

"I suppose so."

They sat in the sun, their elbows companionably bumping as they watched the little boys ride, and the team roping that came afterwards. After that Jordy went to get hamburgers.

He bought the food and walked back to the stands by way of the holding pens. Animals stood with downcast stoicism, constantly picking first one hoof and then another off the cracked, baked dirt. Jordy wiped the sweat away from his eyes and looked over towards the stands, trying to spot Mr. Campbell.

Suddenly his attention was caught by a ragged herd of broncs being driven to the chutes. His heart jumped. He had glimpsed a grey hide and a black mane plunging and tossing in the pack.

He turned and ran along the fenceline, craning his neck to see. The horses formed a single line at the alley. Jordy ran beside them, his heart pounding, the hamburgers crunched in his fists. He pushed through the crowd, his eyes never leaving the grey horse. He got closer, close enough to be sure, and yes, it was his mare and his heart turned over.

She was driven into a chute. Her eyes were big with fear and something more than that. Fight. She bucked and kicked in the tight box that confined her. Her hooves slammed into the boards and she smashed her sides against the chute.

Jordy got behind her chute. He jumped up on the boards, leaned over to see her. "That's my horse!" he cried.

"Beat it, kid!"

"She's my horse! You got my horse in there!"

"Get outta here." The cowboy pushed him.

Jordy raced along the line of chutes looking for someone in charge, yelling, "It's my horse, I found my horse, she's in there!" He grabbed an official-looking man by the arm and shouted, "There's been a mistake. My horse is in your bucking chute!" But the man pushed him away.

Jordy ran back to the mare to make sure she was still there. An unexpected calm came to him. He had found his horse. She belonged to him and he was going to get her back.

Cowboys bent along the row of chutes, checking ropes, adjusting saddles and positioning bucking straps. One by one, they cautiously lowered themselves into the saddles and were catapulted, one by one, into an explosion of riotous spinning and jumping in the bright, bare arena.

Up in the stands, Mr. Campbell wiped the sweat from his brow and squinted at the sun. His head was aching and he wanted to go home. Where was Jordy?

He looked at the next horse. It was rearing and striking at the boards. Its eyes were rolling, the whites showing.

The cowboy grabbed the halter on the horse's head, two men held her head, and the rider dropped onto her back.

He adjusted the rope and leaned back with his legs out front, ready to rake her shoulders with his spurs, ready to go.

The gate swung open. For a heart beat, the horse stood still. Then she reared in the chute and swung herself violently into the boards. The rider lurched back and was tossed off. With a crack and a groan he crashed into the boards as the little grey horse exploded out into the open.

Mr. Campbell leaned forward in the stands, watching the riderless horse. She was bucking like a crazy thing, heedless of fences, outriders, stands. The crowd ooohed. Suddenly, he saw a familiar figure vault over the back of the open chute, leap across the broken body of the rider and run into the blazing barrenness of the arena.

Jordy skidded to a stop in the middle of the ring. He crouched, his arms outstretched, every nerve ready for the right moment. She came towards him like a maniac, plunging, squealing, the halter rope flapping and slapping like a furious snake to one side of her head. She swerved close to him and in an instant he had the rope. It burned through his hands but he held on and she dragged him towards the stands. There were hoofbeats beside him as an outrider raced in, leaned over the mare, and slipped off the bucking cinch. The mare stopped in her tracks, shaking. The boy leaped to his feet. He waved back the riders and the clown, too. He looked steadily at the horse.

It rose out of his heart and spiralled up through the stands towards the sun. In one breath the crowd ceased its murmuring. "Hey-yeh, hey-hey-yeh," Jordy chanted to her.

The horse did not take her eyes from the boy. She snorted and her nostrils flicked in and out as she studied him.

"Hey-hey-yeh, hey-hey." The sound like a caress soothed her. "Siksika, siksika," he murmured. He eased himself towards her, a hand outstretched.

She bobbed her head. Her ears rotated forward. She

stretched her neck towards him, nudged him with her nose.

He stepped to her side and put a hand on the saddle. She veered away. He understood. The saddle had become a bad thing. Carefully he undid it and pulled it off, and like a dancer, in one quick leap was on her bare back. The spell broke and the crowd began to whistle and clap. He urged the mare toward the outgate and the mesmerized crew opened it.

Jordy steered her through the fair grounds, past trailers and campers and nodding cowhorses. He rode her across the highway and away from the town and out onto the prairie, towards home.

Seventeen

MR. CAMPBELL CAME TO LIFE. He scrambled from his seat and rushed down through the stands to the back of the chutes.

"I'm Jeffrey Campbell. Where's the manager? Is there someone in charge here? I must talk to someone." A red-faced cowboy was arguing hotly with two other red-faced men. "Are you in charge here?" He pushed his fishing cap up off his eyebrows.

"Yeah, so what? Who're you?"

"Yes, well, I'm Jeffrey Campbell, I work for the government. I'd like to talk to someone about that boy and the horse he just rode off on."

Instantly a row of sweating cowhands surrounded him, yelling and pointing all at once. Who was that kid? What was he trying to prove?

Mr. Campbell explained to the owner of the broncs. "The boy was given a horse for Christmas," he said. "He trained it, he rode it, he was doing very well. Then it disappeared. Apparently the horse he just rode away on is his horse."

"It's my horse."

"Where did you get it?"

"I bought her from a ranch hand near Calgary."

"Glendon?"

"Yeah. She was beat up pretty bad. He said he found her wild on the range."

"Who said?"

"The guy I got her from."

"Who?"

"I dunno."

"Yes, you do."

"Fred."

"Fred who?"

"Fred sumthin' or other, I dunno."

"I should call the police, don't you think? Let them sort it out."

"Listen, Campbell. She's a good buckin' bronc, just needs to get the hang of comin' out of the chute. I paid good money for her, fair and square. She's worth at least five hundred."

"No, she's not. She nearly killed her rider. She's not worth a dime as a bronc and you know it."

"I could get two hundred for her just as dogfood."

"Two hundred?"

"Yeah."

"I'll give you one hundred."

"Huh?"

"One hundred to take that stolen horse off your mind."

The cowboy spat a wad of tobacco into the dust and swore loudly.

"Deal?"

". . . Deal."

"Good."

Campbell wrote him a cheque and left, a little bounce in his step. He sauntered to his car, got in, leaned his head against the steering wheel, and began to laugh. Jordy had his horse!

The next morning at nine o'clock Mr. Campbell roared into the Blackfoot Reserve. He went to Albert's house and got directions to Jordy's place. Albert went with him.

"Where's my grandson? demanded Joe when the car arrived.

"I'm sorry, Mr. Speckledhawk, I'm sure you've spent an anxious night. I'm afraid Jordy has, well, you see, he found his horse at the rodeo and he rode off on it, and I don't know where he is, although I assume he's headed this way."

"What!"

"Jordy should be home by today."

"He got his horse?"

"Yes, he has." Mr. Campbell beamed.

The three of them sat on the steps and shared a few cups of coffee. They talked a bit and then waited in silence for Jordy. In the late afternoon a horse and a boy appeared, moving slowly on the far side of Ash Creek. Joe noticed first. He stood up and walked without a word to his side of the water. He raised his hands in greeting.

"Grandson!" he called. "Good to see you!"

"Hello grandpa! Good to see you."

Jordy led the mare through the water and took her to the corral. She sniffed at everything until she found the spot she was looking for, lay down, and rolled in the dust. Then she shook herself like a dog after a bath and lay down again with a quiet sigh. For a long time she rested in the shade, facing the river, eyes half closed, an ear occasionally flicking away a pesky fly. Jordy stood nearby, watching her.

"You got her back," said Joe. His eyes were shining.

"Uh huh." The wonder of it was still strong in Jordy and he could barely speak.

"She's hurt. . . ." Joe said.

"I know. She's covered with welts and cuts. See that wire cut across her nose? Somebody beat her up bad." His eyes blazed in outrage.

"Maybe if you looked up Erasmus."

"Yeah."

They walked back to the men sitting on the steps. Mr. Campbell slapped his knees and got up to leave. He stretched and yawned. "Jordy," he said, "there's one problem left over from yesterday."

"Yeah?"

"Well, you see, technically speaking you stole the horse and—"

"What d'ya mean he stole his horse!" Joe cried. "How can a man steal what's his?"

Mr. Campbell ignored Joe, continued looking at Jordy.

"Well, technically you see, uh, well it wasn't your horse and . . . it's just a point of law but the fact remains that I paid a hundred dollars for your horse and . . ."

"You paid for my horse?"

"White men!" Joe snorted and stomped away to the cabin.

After Mr. Campbell had gone, Albert chuckled softly and said, "White men got their own way of doin' things, and Joe's never got used to it. They got a lotta laws, big fat books full of 'em, but they're a bit lean on justice. Don't mean their intentions ain't good, just means somethin' that's simple is likely goin' to be complicated by the time they get through chewin' on it. You know what I mean?"

"Uh . . ."

"Well, you will, you get older." He was quiet for awhile and then he turned, looked at Jordy directly, and touched him firmly on the chest. "You got a source of power," he said softly.

"What do you mean?"

"Power, medicine, you can make things happen, make 'em right."

"Yeah?"

"You should know about it."

"Yeah?"

"You are born with some kinds of power, and you acquire other kinds, maybe from dreams, maybe from spirit helpers, maybe from experience. I don't know how you got yours but I can see it's there."

They sat beneath the shade of the cottonwoods beside the creek. Albert said, "All things in the world have their place, and each one fits together with every other, in harmony. A young boy your age used to go out by himself to seek a vision, to find his place and find his spirit helpers. It was given to some of the people to be healers, or hunters, or dreamspeakers, or warriors. You got to find a vision for

yourself, Jordy. Already you have powerful medicine."
The way the chief explained things, they made sense to
Jordy.

A week later, after he had given the mare a chance to
recover, Jordy rode her to see Erasmus. Erasmus gave him
a supply of dried wormwood sage and explained how to
mix it with sweet grass to make medicine to take away
soreness. He chewed the white flowers of the yarrow plant
and applied it as a poultice to the mare's welts and cuts. He
rubbed a brew of gum plant on her hooves and sprinkled
the powdered leaves of the mountain laurel over her
wire-cut nose. When he was done he looked her over
again, prodding and tapping her as he went. At last he
stood back and said, "She gotta be wormed."

"You got anything for that?"

Erasmus chuckled. "White man's worms require white
man's medicine. See a vet."

Jordy smiled and patted his horse's neck.

"Not much healing needs to be done on the outside a'
this horse," Erasmus said. "The healing that's goin' to take
some time is on the inside. Her spirit's been knocked
around. She needs time."

Eighteen

JUNE CAME TO ITS INEVITABLE END with relieved and rushing students leaping away from the constraints of school. Jordy was glad to see the holidays arrive. Now he was free to concentrate on his mare and on his lessons with Emily.

After their first holiday lesson, Emily pulled a set of papers from a pocket and waved them under Jordy's nose. She waved them at Miss MacTavish too.

"Here they are!" she said, "entry forms for the Alpha Ranch's fifty-mile endurance race. Come on, Jordy. There's a hundred dollar first prize and belt buckles for everyone who finishes! Let's go in the race!"

"My horse's not ready," he said.

"What d'you mean? Look at the forms. It's not until Labor Day. That's two months away. Loads of time!"

In spite of himself, he studied the entry rules. "Couldn't go anyway," he said finally. "Every horse's gotta be under saddle. My horse can't stand a saddle anymore."

"Come on. What d'you say Miss MacTavish?"

"Well, anything can happen in two months," the teacher said. "It wouldn't hurt to enter. Doesn't mean you have to compete if things aren't right in two months. It would sure give you two something to aim for."

"I do need the money." Jordy hesitated. "Well, okay."

"Great!" Emily hollered.

As she drove him home, however, Miss MacTavish was more sober. She remembered the pell-mell pace of the endurance races of her youth, and the thought of Emily caught in the midst of that made her shudder. She turned and looked at Jordy.

"If you take Emily in a race, you must never think about winning. Never! Only about keeping her safe. It's not like a picnic outing."

"I know."

"No, you don't know. You've never been in a race. You two would have to keep to yourselves, away from the pack. If you were ever separated from each other, she would be helpless."

"Uh huh."

"And another thing. Your horse. You must get her used to some sort of saddle again. She's got to learn to lead into a trailer. And have her temperature taken and her hooves and teeth checked, and stand calmly in the midst of chaos while complete strangers check her out."

"Uh huh."

"You've got two months. As for her condition, I don't think that's going to be a problem. She's fit and sound, just a bit stiff and sore. Don't push her and she'll be all right. If anyone's not ready in two months, we'll try for another race later."

"Okay."

"I can coach you, get you all in shape, tell you what you need to know. But when you're out there in the middle of a race, it'll be up to you alone to keep all of you safe."

That night, as Joe sat at his table and stitched, Jordy said, "I'm goin' in a race."

"Yeah?"

"I need a saddle."

"Mare won't be saddled."

"I need a saddle she can accept. Somethin' different. You could make one."

"What? I never made a saddle."

"Yeah. But you could make one anyway."

Joe put down his tools and scratched his head. "What you got in mind?"

"An Indian saddle. One like in the old days. Rules don't say what kind of saddle, just a saddle. You could make an Indian kind."

"I never done one like that. Never even seen one."

"I could find out."

Joe picked up a piece of leather, eyed it, made a cut, put it down, shook his head. "You show me one, I'll do it," he said, and he flashed a smile at Jordy.

Jordy sought out Albert and, just as he'd guessed, the chief came up with directions for an old-time Blackfoot saddle. Albert took the boy to a back room in his store. "This here's my collection of real old stuff," he said. "It ain't like the stuff we wear in parades. . . ." The room was filled with dusty remnants from the lost days of glory—war shirts, shields, lances, medicine bundles, cradleboards—and in the center, the riggings for a war horse—breastplate, bridle, saddle.

Jordy barely breathed. Albert's hand settled on his shoulder. Still, he didn't move. The pride of the Blackfoot nation was hidden here, in this little room. It was a revelation to him.

"Joe could make an old-time saddle like this one," Albert said at last. He tenderly stroked its dusty contours.

"But a new one," Jordy said, "for now."

Their summer days settled into a steady routine of preparation. Joe collected, tanned, and cut leather. He found the proper prairie grasses and dried them for stuffing. Piece by piece, as Joe stuffed it and stitched, the mare's saddle took shape. Jordy spent his days preparing his horse and practicing riding with Emily. Albert taught the mare to trailer. Jordy learned to take her temperature, pulse, and respiration (TPR) rates, and began training her accordingly. The mare learned to accept all this attention with equanimity. Their days were full.

On a hot, still August evening, Jordy took the finished saddle out to the corral and laid it over the top rail. The mare sniffed it and huffed.

"She don't think it looks like a saddle," Joe said, and he chuckled. "She thinks it's a blanket."

The next day, Jordy casually laid it across her back. She

paid no attention. After doing this for a week, one night he cinched it up. She didn't care. He leaped onto her back, for the first time in months settled into a saddle. After riding bareback for so long, his legs were as hard as iron, his grip and balance sure. But this saddle, so softly shaped and light, somehow complimented the rider's position. For the first time, Jordy had a sensation of both closeness with his horse and security in a saddle. He took a deep breath, raised an arm to his grandfather, his pride and confidence bursting.

"We're ready!" he shouted. "We're ready!" and his heart leapt within him.

Nineteen

THE ALPHA RANCH'S LABOR DAY FIFTY-MILE RIDE began
with fifty-two horses plunging onto the trail at the crack of
the starting gun. Jordy watched them go, enjoying the
sight as they raced away. It lifted his spirit to see them so
brim-full ready to run with all the life that was in them.

Jordy's mare danced and fussed, impatient to be off.
Even unflappable Chuck was beginning to sweat and
prance. But Jordy and Emily waited. They knew they
couldn't afford to be swept into a stampede and possibly
separated.

The rumble of hooves diminished. "Let's get going!"
cried Emily. Her cheeks were flushed with excitement.

Jordy laughed. "Hey, yeah!" he yelled and off they went
at a big-moose trot.

Jordy scarcely noticed the fifteen miles to the first vet
check. The going was easy. They passed about half the
competition as Jordy kept them at a methodical, even trot.
Joy burst through Jordy. Beneath him, his horse as solid
and strong as a rock, as steady as an autumn river,
pounded over the earth. Behind him, old, brown Chuck
was gamely keeping pace. His rider, her face taut with
concentration, had settled into a steady rhythm with the
horse. It was glorious. He began to think they could do
anything. And he began to think of winning.

Miss MacTavish had told him to walk the last quarter
mile into each vet check. Now he understood why. By the
time they'd walked a little distance and waited to be
checked by the vet, the pulse and respiration rates of their
horses had returned to near normal. Thus they were
allowed to proceed.

The ten miles to the halfway point were tough. They had to ford a river, wade through a slough and slide down a steep sand cliff. The hardest part was the cliff. As Jordy stopped at the top of it, he turned to Emily and said, "We're at the cliff. Give your horse his head, lean forward, and hang on," and over they went. Emily clutched Chuck's mane and gulped for air.

"Wow!" she gasped at the bottom. Her hands were shaking, her cheeks ashen. For her it had been like plummeting off the edge of the earth, sinking into nothingness.

"You all right?"

She took another breath. "Yeah, I'm okay." She straightened up and grinned. "I made it," she said.

"Let's go then!" They were off again.

When they arrived at the halfway point they were amazed to discover they were in sixth and seventh place. Miss MacTavish ran up to them breathless, pails and sponges in her hands, her eyes shining. As she sponged the horses' legs and heads and let them sip water, she kept up a running monologue of advice. Her students sank into the shade and ate their sandwiches, determined to rest for their mandatory hour-long lunch break. They barely paid attention.

"The second half is always toughest," Miss MacTavish said. "Concentrate on the state of your own horses. Ignore what anyone else is doing. Otherwise your horses will break down."

They set off again at a quiet jog through the rolling ranchlands in the bright afternoon light of a prairie September. Jordy filled his lungs with air and felt the sunshine all through him. He felt good and he could tell his horse did too. He wanted to run towards the sun, keep running until he could go straight into its yellow roundness.

"Let's pick it up, move out!" he called back to Emily. He increased the tempo of his horse's trot. "Hey-yeh-hey," he chanted softly, his song holding them all together.

They were trotting across a stretch of flat, unbroken prairie. Jordy's mare was going strong and he had not noticed that Chuck was beginning to tire. Ahead, he could see a group of horses walking and he decided to pass them. The mare stretched out, lengthened her stride, and broke into a run.

He turned to look at Emily when suddenly, his horse was flying through the air. Before he'd landed or could think to warn Emily, Chuck was also jumping over the drainage ditch Jordy had failed to notice. But Emily wasn't. She had crashed into the ground with a bone-wrenching thud.

Chuck stopped. The mare stopped too. Jordy leaped to the ground and ran to her. His heart pounded alarm into his ears because she looked so small and broken. He knelt beside her and cradled her head in his arms. Emily clutched her sides, her eyes tightly shut, tears squeezing out of the corners.

"Emily?" he whispered.

She took a deep breath and began to sob. They were big, lurching sobs and Jordy's heart broke to hear them.

"I'm so scared," she said. "I'll never be anything."

"What?"

"We won't finish. Jordy, I'm so sorry," she cried.

He didn't know what to say. Silently, he cradled her.

"I thought I could do it, I thought I could do anything but I'm so scared! I can't! I can't!"

Chuck had picked his way across the ditch. He reached down with his nose to nudge her. His soft breath touched her face and fluttered her hair. She raised a hand to pat him and recoiled with a groan.

"Oh," she whispered, "it hurts so bad."

"What's the matter?"

"My side . . . I think I might have cracked some ribs."

Soundlessly, her tears streamed down her cheeks. Jordy could feel a tenderness stirring in him he'd never felt before. He took her face in his hands.

"You can do anything," he said.

"No I can't. I'm scared, Jordy. Everything was out of control and I was helpless. I couldn't ride a horse if you weren't with me. I just tag along. I can't do anything just myself."

"Yes you can."

"I can't!"

"Stand up," he said. He carefully set her on her feet. "Go find your horse," and he backed away.

"Jordy? . . . Smarten UP! . . . You! . . . You!"

"Make up your mind. Find him."

In spite of herself, Emily tilted her head to one side, trying to catch a sound, a clue to Chuck's position. The horse moved a step as he grazed. She could feel the shifting weight of him through the earth. She could hear the bridle jingle as he bit a tuft of grass. Carefully, slowly, she went to him, reached out her hands, and touched his quiet side.

"Get on him."

"Oh sure."

"Do it."

She held the reins, grasped the saddle horn, and raised her left foot to the stirrup. Pain shot through her but she hoisted herself into the saddle anyway.

"Let's finish the race," she said. "You coming?"

"Uh huh." Jordy moved the horses out and back onto the trail.

Chuck had had enough and by now it was obvious. He had managed to keep up for forty miles, but he had run out of energy. They walked. Riders passed them. It didn't matter. Miles went by before the older horse was ready to trot. But Emily couldn't stand the jar of it. By this time the pain in her side had worn her out. Ashen-faced and barely breathing, however, she refused to quit.

They reached the finish line last. The sun was setting and the winner had already been loaded into the trailer and was on the way home. Miss MacTavish ran to them and helped Emily off her horse.

"What's the matter?" she gasped.

"She's hurt," Jordy said. "I shouldn't have made her do it."

"Oh shut up, Jordy," Emily retorted.

"What happened?"

"She fell. She's hurt real bad and I made her go on."

"You did not. It was none of your business. I made me go on."

"What happened?"

Jordy told her. Miss MacTavish's usually perky features clouded over. She was about to speak when the vet came toward them and handed her the final checklist along with the ones from the other three vet checks. He regarded Emily with concern.

"You look in rough shape," he said. "Anything I can do to help?"

"I'll be okay. Just tell us how the horses did."

"Well, the bay quarterhorse certainly isn't cut out for this sort of thing." He paused and studied Jordy and the mare carefully. "But, young man, that little horse you have shows tremendous potential. Her TPRs are exceptional, her recovery excellent. . . . I think you may have a winner on your hands."

At the moment Jordy felt like anything but a winner, and the vet's words made no impression.

"I'd like to recommend you be invited to ride in the Hallman Cup Ride."

"What's that?" he asked.

"It's Canada's biggest endurance race. It draws outstanding horses from Canada and the U.S.—100 miles in one day, near Jasper. Would you be interested?"

"I don't know," Jordy said tiredly.

"Yes, we're interested." Miss MacTavish's eyes were bright.

"Okay, I'll have the committee send you the papers." The vet looked at the boy quizzically. "By the way," he said, "your saddle got a lot of attention today, among the judges and the racers. It seems to have held up very well. I've never seen one like it."

"It's a Blackfoot saddle."

Jordy was very quiet on the ride home. Emily's fall had sent a shock of guilt reverberating through his system. He remembered Albert's story about the first duty of a Blackfoot man. He was depressed and discouraged. The three of them sat cramped and quiet in the cab of MacKenzie's truck and said nothing until they were back at Emily's.

"I shoulda gone easy, like you said," Jordy said. "Emily wouldn't have fallen."

"It was an accident. . . . So what? . . . Forget it," Emily said.

Jordy didn't answer. Still, his fingers found the silver buckle the ride officials had given him, and he rubbed its shiny face. Here was the proof that at least they'd finished the course. At least they'd done that much.

"Jordy," Emily softly said, "thank you. We got through a race. Just you and me. I'll remember it all my life."

"Huh."

She poked him in the ribs and got out of the truck. As her father led her away to the house she turned and called out in a voice charged with joy, "Hallman Cup, here we come!"

Twenty

SCHOOL BEGAN AGAIN with dreary predictability. The first day back, Jordy's English teacher assigned a page of writing on "Summer Memories," his socials teacher handed out texts and told everyone to read chapter one, his math teacher was ready with a trick-quiz review, and his science teacher talked for an hour about getting work done on time. Jordy's only relief was that Miss MacTavish took her class out for baseball. Jordy stared out windows most of the day, remembering the excitement of the race. He could summon no interest in school nor imagine any reason to be there. By the end of the week he was numb with boredom.

On Saturday he took his horse for a long ride, lost himself in the rolling stretches of golden grassland. Out on the prairie, with his horse beneath him, he felt like his real self again. And the mare, no longer held up by the slower Chuck, let loose the power she contained, romped and ran for miles.

It was late afternoon when they made their way up Main Street on their way home. Jordy picked up the mail. There were two letters, one for Joe, one for him. He whistled softly as he read his. They ambled up the street to the school, and Jordy got off the mare and knocked at the old teacher's door.

"How nice to see you!" she said. "Come in. Let me make you tea."

He tied the horse to her front porch and went inside. "I don't want to go to school," he said. "I want to work around here, not sit all day in Glendon."

"Oh."

"But I'd like to finish school. Can you tell me about correspondence courses?"

She told him. She added, "Your mother took a lot of courses this way and did very well. I'm sure you'd have no trouble."

"Did you know my mother well?"

"Yes, I did. Sarah was a lovely girl."

"Did people like her?"

"Everyone loved her."

"Yeah, but white men ... uh ..." Jordy's stomach felt like a twisted balloon. There was one thing he wanted to know now. He blurted, "Who killed her?"

Miss Hind went to a filing cabinet beside her desk and patted its grey top. "Blackfoot archives," she said, and pulled out several sheets of yellowed, brittle newspaper. Wordlessly, she handed them to Jordy and sat down beside him.

While the crickets chittered and the children down the street laughed and played, Jordy read. It was his grandfather who had made the headlines. The paper said a "knife-wielding renegade" had stormed into a bar and gutted a white man. There was a picture of his grandfather, manacled, surrounded by mounties, getting into a squad car. There was a picture of the murdered man as well, and Jordy's eyes jumped at the name under the face: John Brady. The dead man's brother, Fred, demanded justice be done.

"Do you know how it happened?" Jordy asked.

Miss Hind put her teacup down and folded her hands in her lap. Her rocking chair creaked back and forth, a counterpoint to the crickets and the distant, squealing children. Her eyes looked far away.

"At the time I heard all kinds of stories, but all I know for sure is that she was attacked as she was walking home alone from a dance. . . . Perhaps you don't know, but some of the white boys around here had the notion that Indian girls were fair game; they could do anything they wanted and it didn't matter. It was not uncommon for girls to be attacked. Nothing was ever done about the attackers until your grandfather fixed up one of them, permanently." She said this with some satisfaction, as if she considered justice to have been served.

Jordy sat in wretched silence and stared out the window for a long time. He thought about how unfair life was and about how much he hated Fred. He thought about getting even.

The sun was low in the sky. A meadowlark's bright song trilled clearly over the sounds of insects, children, and swings. For an instant, Jordy saw the bird flitting over the prairie. He forced his thoughts to the present. He pulled a piece of paper out of his pocket, unfolded it, and handed it to the old teacher.

She studied it carefully. It was an invitation. The officials of the Hallman Ride hoped he would attend their contest and take a run at the prizes: a trophy and a thousand dollars for the first horse, a trophy for the best conditioned horse, and one hundred dollars for each of the top ten finishers. They had enclosed entry forms for the Thanksgiving Day race.

"It must be an honour for them to ask you," she said.

"I guess. . . . I need the money to pay back a debt."

"It would bring honor to your family and your people for you to go and do your best." She looked at him and nodded. "I think you should go. I think you should win it."

Jordy arrived home with a mixture of thoughts competing inside him. Thoughts of his mother, Fred Brady, Joe, the horse, and the race were tangled in a terrible knot. Feelings of hatred, anger, ambition, fear, and pride all had a grip on his heart. He handed his grandfather's letter to him in silence.

Joe read his letter and grinned. "Huh!" he said. "Some guy likes the saddle I made, wants me to make him one."

"That's good. . . . I'm goin' in another race."

"Yeah?"

"I gotta work a lot on my horse. . . . I'm not goin' back to school."

"What? You gotta have book learnin'!"

"I know, grandpa." He explained about correspondence. After a lot of explaining, the old man finally nodded. It was all right if Jordy stayed home as long as he continued his education. Joe showed the boy his letter and wondered out loud if he could turn this into a new business. Both of them smiled to think how easily their lives could change direction.

Jordy quit school and turned his attention to conditioning the mare for the big race. Miss MacTavish gave him books to read on the subject and sent him with all his questions to the Calgary library.

"For someone who don't go to school anymore, you sure loaded with books," Joe said with a chuckle.

Jordy wormed the mare again and put her on a special diet. He got a notebook and kept track of all her workouts, her distances, her times, her TPRs and recovery rates. On weekends the MacKenzies trailered the boy and horse to the mountains and he worked the mare uphill hard.

The mare thrived. The more work she was given, the stronger she got. After a month she could cover fifty miles in four hours with ease.

The week before the race was a week of rest. Jordy worked her lightly, took her out to graze. He let Miss MacTavish worry about the details of equipment, crews, timetables, and strategy.

On Thursday he walked the mare to Main Street to get the mail. He stopped at Miss Hind's. Miss Hind grinned at them.

"My dear," she said, "you both look wonderful! Iron-fit! Come in for tea."

When he was settled at her table and she had brought him tea, he showed her the package from the post office.

"It's the correspondence stuff," he said with a sigh. The sight of its heavy bulk made him wonder why he was doing this. "I might need some help."

"You might."

"I like learnin' about stuff that's interesting."

"I know what you mean. There are different kinds of education, different ways of learning. It doesn't have to be out of a book. The main thing is that whatever you set your mind to, you never stop learning about it."

"Yeah."

"I used to help your mother with her courses."

"Could you help me?"

"I'd like that very much."

He rode home feeling light and happy. The thought came to him that he *was* home. The reserve, grandpa, these Blackfoot people, everything was in place at last. Everything was fine. He thought of the race on Monday and he felt a spring of determination bubble up inside him. He wanted to win!

Twenty-One

ERASMUS LEANED OVER THE STALL DOOR and looked in at the mare. The reporter stood on his toes and looked in, too.

"Doesn't look like a contender to me," he said.

"Huh."

"Says on the list her name is 'Horse'. What kind of a name is that?"

Erasmus shook his head and edged away.

"Who are you? Are you the trainer?"

Erasmus picked up the water bucket and walked away. For a moment he regretted coming to this race. He hated the hustle and the hype. It was a big event and the national news, the national magazines, and all the western papers gave it lots of coverage. He would rather be home, away from pecky little people like that newsman, who even now was furiously scribbling in his dog-eared notebook. But something about the boy and the mare had touched him and he was resolved to do whatever he could for them. It would all be over tomorrow anyway and then he could go home. He filled the bucket and took it back to the mare. She was quiet and relaxed, and as she sloshed her nose in the water, he scratched her side and wondered when Jordy would be back from the pre-ride orientation.

The ride was going to be a rugged test covering 100 miles of mountain trails and prairie roads. Eighty-seven riders expected to race their horses across it in under twenty hours and about half of them thought they had a chance of winning.

By the time Jordy left the orientation meeting, he was sure *he* didn't stand a chance. The young woman who sat beside him had already won three fifty-milers and a one-hundred-mile ride earlier in the year on a twenty-thousand-dollar Arabian stallion called Abdul al Aba, Bub for short. A man sitting in front of him had won this ride last year on an Arab-Appaloosa cross called Frankey and was back to duplicate the feat. Another lady had trailered her Morgan gelding all the way from California to compete in the premier Canadian contest. She let it be known that she had won several regional championships in the States and wanted to see how the competition up north rated. Her horse, Donovan's Dandy, was a pro, she said. And there were others whose experience and demeanor had thoroughly unnerved him. It seemed everyone there was a seasoned rider on an impressively expensive, well-bred horse. Jordy figured he would be lucky if he even finished.

He went back to the barn for one last check on his horse. He slumped down in the hay at her feet and barely noticed when Erasmus poked his head into the stall.

"What's wrong?" the big man asked.

"I don't stand a chance," Jordy said glumly.

"How's that?"

"Everyone's got such fast horses, they've done this a lot, and they're winners. Their horses cost a fortune and . . ."

"Hell kid, every horse's got four legs, heart and lungs, and a brain the size of a small tomato. Don't matter when the chips are down what some dummy paid for it."

"Yeah but—"

"Listen, kid. You feelin' bad 'cause your horse wasn't born in an air-conditioned stall and babied half her life? You don't know nuthin'. Your horse already got goin' for her the best advantage a horse could have in this kind of race."

"Yeah?"

"You want a winner in this sorta thing, first thing you need is toughness. Your mare was born tough else she'd never have survived. She lived tough. For her it's never been any big deal to cover fifty, a hundred miles a day, hard goin', little food, little water. She's been endurin' all her natural life. Mental-wise, that puts her miles ahead of some of these pampered pussycats."

"Yeah but—"

"Kid, don't exasperate me. I looked at just about all these nags here. Only about four you need to worry about."

Jordy sighed. What did Erasmus know? He hadn't been to the meeting. He hadn't heard the competition. He was just an old man from the back woods. Still, there was a ring of authority in his voice that was comforting to hear.

"Think of this, Jordy," Erasmus said. "While most of these other horses were standin' around tame little pastures growin' fat, your horse was runnin' miles and miles every day, growin' bone and muscle and heart. She's been runnin' up and down mountains all her life. Why, she was fitter when she was a yearling than half these animals are now."

"I guess so."

"Have some faith, kid."

Jordy stretched and got up. He patted the mare. However well he did tomorrow, he knew she was a good horse, and he loved her.

"I'm tired," he said.

"Go get some sleep. I'm stayin' with the horse."

Jordy was met at the motel by Emily and his crew. Miss MacTavish was the boss. She outlined strategy and everyone's duties. Albert and Joe would meet him at the twenty- and eighty-mile vet checks, while Miss MacTavish and Erasmus would look after things at the halfway point. Everyone checked over his or her lists of equipment— everything from hoofpicks to ice packs—and reviewed what had to be done.

As for strategy, Miss MacTavish figured they might make the top ten if Jordy kept a steady eight-miles-per-hour pace, saved as much horse energy as he could, and pushed the mare a little towards the end. Jordy had no idea that every rider there considered a top ten finish sufficient glory for any one-hundred-mile race. He wanted to know who he had to beat to win.

"Well," the teacher said, "I wouldn't try too hard to win. We don't really know how much your horse has got; we've never pushed her to the limit before, and frankly, if you push her beyond her limit, she'll break down and you won't even finish. You've got to really pay attention to how she's coping with the stress. The first thirty miles, climbing up into the mountains, are the toughest, and a lot of horses will bog down there. That's where you've got to save horse, go easy. Once you're in the mountains, you catch up if you need to, go steady. When you start coming down, the temptation is to speed up. Don't. The last twenty miles will be fast. The contenders will turn on the juice and that's when you'll find out how much heart this horse has."

"Yeah, but who've I gotta beat?"

She groaned, sure he was going to blow any chance of finishing.

"Okay," she said, "I'll tell you who the pros are. They have excellent horses and if you get too close, they'll try to throw you and your horse off the pace you need to keep." She scanned the list of entries.

"There's Karen Jawarski riding Abdul al Aba. That horse is incredibly strong. And Jack Marsdale with Frankey; they won last year. That horse is tough. Simone Rettinger on the Dandy; I've heard they're good. I also think Harvey Lawson has a good chance. He's riding an Arab mare called Dollie, and Doug Jenkins is riding a good horse this year, a half-Arab called Desert Poco. They'll be up front. And there's one more you have to watch for." She stopped, put the paper down, and looked at Jordy. "Fred Brady is here. He's riding an Arab stallion called Neferrez. He's shooting his mouth off, Jordy. He says you'll never race, never finish. Be on your guard. Okay?"

"Okay."

She patted his arm and suggested everyone get some sleep. They would all be up before dawn and Jordy would be off and running by 5:00 A.M.

They all said good night and went to their rooms. Emily got into bed, pulled the blankets over her head, tried to sleep. It was no use. All the way up from Calgary, she had played Beethoven tapes on the truck's stereo system and those mighty strains still rumbled through her head and would not let her sleep.

Across the room, Jane MacTavish went over and over the lists of equipment, horses, and riders. Her stubborn brain refused to sleep, insisted, instead, on pouring over every combination of possibilities that tomorrow's events might bring. She imagined a hundred situations and, in all of them, there was something that could go wrong.

In the next room, Albert and Joe had their own thoughts to keep them awake. Albert had funded this venture with money from the tribe and he was anxious about it. If the boy didn't even finish, the tribal grumblers would bellyache about throwing money around. If Jordy did well, Albert himself would be congratulated for furthering the cause of tribal pride and public image.

Joe was also thinking about pride. He was remembering when a certain pride had first touched him. He had been lying on his prison cot in the dark, and from some cell on his tier an explosion of tempers had erupted. Someone had screamed. Bodies had slammed against bars, fists had pounded into flesh and furniture crashed. Guards rushed in. Cracks and muffled groans and the sounds of feet dragging signalled the end of the disturbance. Then voices shredded the silence, "Useless Indians, bloody scum, we'll put you away for good." Someone laughed, a laugh as brittle as dead skin. It was then, as Joe lay on his narrow prison bed, that a sense of beauty, an unexpected pride had come to him. He was an Indian. Indians were not scum. From that day, he had declared that pride with the one mark of Indianness available to him. Hair. For Indians it had always been regarded as an extension of the soul, a symbol of holiness. For Joe it became a declaration of his pride. But this pride was also connected to his growing hatred of white man things. And now the hatred no longer felt good. He longed to be free of it.

In the barn Erasmus stirred at the sound of footsteps approaching. He stretched his legs in the sawdust and looked up at the mare. Her ears were pricked forward, her eyes widened, and she edged nervously towards the back of the stall. Then Erasmus could hear the low murmur of voices as walkers approached. He got a faint whiff of wine and beer. The mare was trembling. Someone came to a halt at the mare's door and someone chuckled, "Here's one for ya, ya little bastard, one less ya owe me for." As Erasmus crouched inside the stall and watched the half-door, a hand reached over and poured something into the water bucket.

Quick as a cat, Erasmus grabbed the hand, pulled down, and twisted. Its owner yelled and struggled to release himself. Another set of arms reached over the door and collared Erasmus in a head-lock and then he was hit on the head. He fell back. The arms loosened, footsteps retreated, the little horse snorted in terror.

Slowly Erasmus picked himself up, rubbed his aching neck. He went to the horse and eventually calmed her. He threw out the water, filled another bucket, and once more bedded down with the mare. But he could not sleep. He remained alert and tense the rest of the night.

As for Jordy, he sat on the edge of his bed and tried to relax but it was hopeless. A host of thoughts and worries crowded into his head. He hoped he could win enough money to pay back Mr. Campbell. He wondered if he would be tough enough to last a hundred miles. He worried about Fred Brady. He worried about going off course, about accidents, and about other riders. Would he be able to pace his horse properly? What if she broke down? There were so many things he had yet to find out. Two things he knew for sure: he was glad he was here with the mare, and he was going to give it his best shot.

Twenty-Two

IN THE FRAGILE PREDAWN LIGHT the saddle took on an aura of antiquity. It was as though its ancient form was evidence of an unseen reality, another world hovering about it. When Joe looked at it he could almost hear the vanished buffalo rumbling over the prairie and the yips and hoots of the pursuing hunters. He let his gnarled fingers linger over it before he lifted it onto the back of Jordy's horse. It was his creation of softness and strength, and somehow, when it was on the mare, she seemed more than just herself. She was a presence from that other age.

Jordy slipped the bridle on over the halter and scratched the horse around the ears. She rubbed her head against him and nudged him gently. He took a deep breath, patted her once, and led her out into the dark.

He was glad Joe was with him now. Horses and people on the starting grounds were moving between timers, vets, officials, trailers, and buckets in a kind of slow motion float. The TV lighting that the camera crews had set up lent a sense of magic to the scene. Jordy felt a moment of panic.

Then Miss MacTavish was in front of him, putting his number on him, delivering reminders about all the things he knew anyway.

"You're number twenty-seven," she said. "You leave in the third group at 5:10, so there's a little time to wait." She tried to smile but the crease in her brow belied her tenseness. "The main thing is to stay loose, transmit relaxation to your horse. If you get uptight so will she. Okay?" She eyed him intently.

"Okay." He took a deep breath, tried to feel loose, but it was no use; his heart was racing.

"Ah hell," chimed in Joe, "you been doin' long rides long enough now. Just pretend you're goin' cross country to see Emily. No big deal. All this fuss is ridiculous."

"Where is Emily?" Jordy asked.

"With Albert at the starting line," Miss MacTavish assured him. "She'll be with me all day."

The announcer called the first group to the starting line and, when they were ready, sent them off with a crisp "Go!" Ten riders headed down the trail at a calm, easy trot. Karen on the Arab, Bub, and Jack on Frankey led the way, the picture of unruffled purpose.

The next group assembled at the line and waited. Fred Brady was among them, sitting on his horse with a slight tilt to one side. The timers checked their sheets, and at 5:05 the announcer said, "Go!" Fred's horse took off at a big bounding canter. The rest moved out at a trot.

Then it was Jordy's turn. He settled into the saddle and walked the mare to the start. He heard the TV announcer off to one side speaking into his mike about the point of interest in this group being an Indian boy on an Indian mustang using an Indian saddle. Not contenders. A human interest touch. The wide face of the camera swung in his direction. Jordy searched the crowd for a familiar face, one last reassuring bit of advice. For an instant he spotted Emily. He longed to talk to her.

"Go!"

Before he had time to think, they were off. The mare moved out in a big, free trot and, to his surprise, he found himself at the head of his group. Behind him he could hear the American softly chanting, "Easy-easy" to her big Morgan. The others in the group faded to the background as the leaders began the long climb into the mountains.

He knew the mountains were seven miles away and he planned to be in them within the hour. He was not surprised to be passing horses before then. Miss Mac-Tavish had explained that there were really two events going on, two classes of horses and riders. There were those who were out to win and there were those who simply enjoyed participating, whose sole ambition was to complete the ride in decent shape.

Ahead of him, the mountains seemed to hang suspended in the dawn mist. He could feel his heart reach out to them and an exhilaration filled him.

"Hey Yeaaaah!" he yelled, and he swung his head and urged the mare to extend herself. Behind him, he could sense the Morgan catch fire and come roaring up to them. Head to head, the little mustang and the Morgan trotted through the hills towards the mountains. Jordy glanced at Simone.

In a moment she began to slow her horse, humming, "That's a Dandy, that's a boy." Jordy eased his horse back to an easy jog and, together, the four of them made it into the mountains in good time.

"Good horse you got," said Simone when they had slowed to a walk. She kept her horse beside Jordy, eyeing the two of them, frankly curious. "What kind of saddle is that?" she asked.

Jordy smiled. "Blackfoot. Not many around."

She smiled. "It looks comfortable."

"Yeah."

"Well, I must be off," she said. She gave her horse an almost imperceptible nudge and a cluck and he set off up the steep rocky trail at a canter.

Jordy hesitated for a moment. Should he follow at a similar pace? He peered up the trail. The dawn's light was laying its first touch on the edges of the trees bordering the path. Flecks of burnished gold sprinkled themselves across the rocking backs of the American and her horse as they disappeared up the path. He remembered what Miss MacTavish had said: "Ride your own race," and he decided that he would do as he always did when going up steep inclines. He urged the mare forward at an energetic trot and up they went into the timber.

The rocks and ruts on the trail made the going tricky

and, by the time they had climbed a mile, Jordy was breathing hard and so was the horse. They walked on for a hundred metres, around a curve in the trail, and suddenly, the forest opened into a meadow. A few riders and their mounts were already on the other side. He could see the Dandy as he cantered into the dark of the woods on the far side. The American and the Morgan were setting quite a pace. And he hadn't yet caught a glimpse of the fast ones in the first two groups. They could be miles ahead. He decided then that there was no way he could win. He relaxed. He would ride a good race and enjoy himself. It occurred to him that finishing in the top ten would be quite an accomplishment.

It was then that the mare began to dance beneath him. She was no stranger to alpine meadows. She tossed her head and whinnied and, without his bidding, broke into a bounding canter that took them across the meadow before the startled Jordy could gather his wits. He grinned with delight and let his body move in rhythm to her running. In no time, they were alongside the Morgan once again. "Hi!" he said to Simone.

She looked surprised. She hadn't expected to see the kid and his rangy pony again. A frown creased her face. She nodded to him and urged her horse ahead.

Jordy, on the other hand, had been pleased to see how, if he held true to his own pace, his horse could keep up. He slowed the mare to a quiet jog and let the other horse steam ahead. There were about seven miles to the first vet check and he didn't want the mare winded or tired by the time they reached it. Not with another eighty miles to go.

He filled his lungs with crisp mountain air. Sunlight was now taking command of the sky and the earth, giving everything it touched a vibrance it had not possessed before. He rode to the ridge above and stopped for a moment. To the east were the hills and plains stretching away to the sun; to the west the wall of rock and timber reached upward. On the one side, an openness of pale gold and dusty green; on the other, the dark mass of the mountain.

The earth at that moment seemed new to him—the sight of the prairie from here, the texture of the air, the mountain scents riding the wind. Even colours had a new brilliance in this crackling air. He didn't want to move it was so beautiful.

He heard the clattering hoofbeats and labored breathing of horses coming up the trail behind him. "Let's go," he whispered and he headed the horse up to the next ridge. For awhile the trail levelled out and they cantered easily along it. They crossed a stream and clambered up a cliff and by breakfast, arrived at the twenty-mile vet stop, high in the mountains.

"7:31," the timer wrote on her timesheet beside number twenty-seven. A veterinarian and his assistant quickly examined the mare and recorded her temperature, pulse and respiration rates. The TPRs were a bit high and Jordy was given ten minutes to get them down.

"Hi Jordy." Albert's comfortable bulk was beside him, helping him with the horse. Joe appeared with sponges and buckets of water. The two men busied themselves with the mare and left the boy to sink to the ground and eat. He leaned his head against the craggy bark of a tree and watched them cool out the horse.

People and horses were everywhere. Several horses arrived at the first vet check plainly exhausted, and were disqualified. One had thrown a shoe and cracked a hoof and was taken out of the race. Most were checked and judged healthy enough to continue.

It wasn't long before the mare was declared ready and Jordy was off with a clatter of hooves and a chorus of encouragement. He settled into the saddle, glad to be on the trail again.

The route shifted further back into the mountains, then wound around a mountain and back out to the foothills. The horse breezed along. Jordy could feel her heartbeat, its steady strength a song of joy for him to sing with.

"Hey-yeh, hey-yeh," his song carried them over the mountain.

Ten miles from the halfway stop, Jordy passed Fred Brady. The Arab stallion was in a lather and jigging, tossing his elegant head and banging his teeth together in time to his agitated prancing. Jordy let the little mare fly past them, but he didn't miss the look of surprise and then hatred that crossed the man's face. He knew Brady couldn't bring his horse into a vet check in such a lather. He would have to go slowly until the horse loosened up. Jordy grinned despite the little prickling fear that always crawled up his back whenever he saw the ex-foreman.

He looked at his watch. He was startled to see that he was considerably ahead of schedule. With sixty miles still to go he knew he must guard his horse's energy. He slowed her down. "Hey-hey-yeh," he crooned and let her walk.

There weren't many horses at the halfway stop when Jordy arrived. Miss MacTavish bounded up to him, her eyes as wide as silver dollars, a trail of supplies flapping behind her.

"Jordy! Gee!" she exclaimed. "What're you doing here so soon?"

What could he say? The mare had felt so good, she had just zipped along. "She's loose, she's goin' easy," he said.

"Gee!"

"Hi kid," said Erasmus. "Might as well get off her. Your turn at the vet's next." His face had a definite I-told-you-so cast to it.

The timer rushed up to them and recorded the time: 10:45. She escorted the horse to the vet, who checked legs and feet and TPRs.

"Good enough," she said.

"You may leave at 11:45," said the timer.

"Gee!" MacTavish muttered under her breath.

While Erasmus groomed the horse and let her eat hay and some salted biscuits he had concocted, Miss Mac-Tavish huddled beside Jordy, watching the other horses come in. Miss MacTavish was afraid Jordy was pushing the horse too fast. "It's a common mistake beginners make," she said. "It's all very well that you're doing so well, but if you burn her out now, there'll be nothing left for the finish." Jordy shrugged questioningly. The horse seemed to get stronger the further they went. What was he supposed to do? "Let up at the first sign of fatigue or dullness," she said. "Don't blow it." She reviewed with him all the tell-tale signs of fatigue. He ate a hamburger and listened to every word. Emily sat beside him, leaned lightly against his arm, and said nothing.

Ten minutes before Jordy was to leave, Fred Brady arrived. A couple of minutes later a flush-faced official skidded to a halt in front of Miss MacTavish and declared that a complaint had been lodged against Jordy. Brady was saying that Jordy had fouled his horse—that was the reason it was so hot and flustered.

"That isn't so!" Jordy yelled. "That isn't fair!"

The official eyed him skeptically.

"I know Fred Brady," Emily said. "He used to work for us. He's been after Jordy all year."

"I don't know," the official said. There were four minutes left before Jordy was to leave.

"Look," Miss MacTavish said. "let Jordy continue. At the end of the race you can verify that this guy has been threatening the boy. I'm sure the only conclusion you'll reach is that the charge is a lie. In the meantime, it's only fair that my rider be allowed to continue."

"Well . . . I . . ."

"What else can you do?"

There was one minute left before he should go.

"Of course I'm right."

"Well. Go."

As Jordy vaulted onto his horse, the timer called after him, "I'll have to check it out!"

"Good luck!" Emily called.

It took Jordy a mile or two to settle down. When the flood of adrenalin had subsided, he realized he was pushing the horse too fast and he slowed to a walk.

"Relax," he told himself. But his stomach was in such a knot he had to stop to throw up.

After awhile he forgot about winning or losing, forgot about Brady. He concentrated on the rhythm of the horse's breathing and they trotted along for miles.

He couldn't know that Brady's complaint was disallowed, or that Brady had left the halfway stop in a rage, his only thought to get Jordy. So he was caught by surprise when Fred roared up behind him on his frantic horse.

"Hey, you little bastard!" Fred yelled. "Just you and me now kid. I'm gonna teachya a lesson!" He struck the stallion with his whip to drive him alongside the mare.

At the sound of Brady's voice, the mare reared and bolted out of control. The stallion took off after her. The two horses charged down the trail, eyes rolling, mouths frothing, sweat flying in flecks from their driving shoulders.

They raced down the mountain and around a curve. The trail was steep. It dropped away to the right of them. Heedless, Fred compelled his horse onward, lashing its heaving sides with his whip. The stallion surged alongside the mare and Brady reached over and smashed the whip across Jordy's face. The mare panicked and leaped into the path of the stallion.

He tripped and fell. His beautiful muzzle skidded into the dirt. His knees cracked under the force of his fall and he flipped heavily onto his side.

For an instant Brady hung suspended in space, then tumbled without a sound over the cliff.

Jordy brought his terrified horse to a halt. Blood was pouring out of his nose, and he saw through a haze. Regardless, he jumped down and went to stand by the mare's head. Her sides were heaving and her eyes were wild with fright.

"Hey-hey, eeasy," he whispered. "It's okay, it's okay."

It wasn't the least bit okay; he could tell that right away. He crooned to her. Sound. Soft, easy sound was what was needed.

It was plain to him that they'd blown the race. The mare was winded. He checked out her legs. Everything seemed sound. At least she could walk to the next vet check.

He wiped the blood from his face and chest and rubbed his eyes. A sound intruded itself on his consciousness, a sound he could not identify. He shook his head. It came again, a sort of rasping moan. He turned.

The stallion had been trying to get up but he lay still now, his head raised and turned toward Jordy, a desperate plea in his eyes. Jordy tied his own horse to a bush and went to him. He could see the broken skin on the knees and the thick blood oozing out of them. He knew the horse was finished and he couldn't do a thing for him—not make it easier for him, not even put him out of his misery. He sat down and cradled the horse's head and he cried.

Presently he became aware of another sound, a groan and then a whimper. He supposed it must be Brady. At that moment Jordy hated Brady with a pure and terrible hatred. The fate of his mother and the fate of the stallion came together in his mind, both helpless victims of the same viciousness. He wanted to kill the man.

The stallion groaned and laid his head on the ground. Jordy got up and went to the edge of the cliff and peered over. Ten meters down, Brady was sprawled on a bush that grew out of the cliff face over a long drop to a creek bed. One slip or one push and the man would be gone. Jordy started down the gravelly cliff to the helpless Brady.

Brady was stunned. He had cracked his ribs and smashed his head. He groaned and fumbled with the bush that held him, dumbly trying to get away. Then, in front of his eyes, the face appeared, and he made a fumbling attempt to grab it.

Fred began to whine. "You got a knife? You gonna get me like your old man got my brother?" he whimpered. He closed his eyes and coughed a bloody gurgle.

The flood of hate that had surged through Jordy drained away. Brady was at his mercy. He couldn't hurt him. "I'll help you," he said.

Jordy extended his hand. Brady grabbed it, as dumbly as he had tried to grab the face a moment before, and Jordy pulled and dragged and pushed him up the bank.

Fred had passed out by the time Jordy got him back on the trail. Jordy flopped him down not far from the crippled stallion. He waited until a rider appeared who promised to report the situation at the next vet check and send out an emergency crew and someone with a gun.

Jordy turned to the mare. She was breathing regularly now and looking better. He took heart. Brady regained consciousness. "There's your horse," said Jordy. "Look after him." He mounted the mare and rode off.

They walked for a mile. Other horses passed them but Jordy didn't care. His horse was all right, and that was all that mattered. In a little while the mare seemed to brighten up. She broke into a sedate trot and Jordy let her. With the rhythm of the trot, her strength returned to her and, by the time they came into the eighty-mile checkpoint, she had her second wind.

"What happened to you?" Albert asked.

"The horse is okay but I don't know about the rider," said the vet. "I'm only supposed to check the horses." He scratched his head. "You don't look too good, son."

"I'm all right," Jordy replied. As long as the horse was in good shape, nothing was going to prevent him from continuing.

He remembered something Emily had said to him after the Alpha ride. She had tried to cheer him up, let him know what she thought of him, and she had said, "Losers don't try. Winners don't quit. We won, Jordy. We did."

"I won't quit," he said to the vet and he mounted his horse.

Twenty miles to go. Despite his aching muscles and empty stomach, Jordy felt happy. They were going to finish and that was something to be proud of. By now dusk was casting blue shadows over the trail. The little mare surged forward with renewed vigor.

But exhaustion was taking over Jordy. The pain in his

face was getting worse and his legs were beginning to shake. So what, he thought. It must have been worse than this for Emily. He told himself he could do what she had done.

He was surprised when they passed a horse. It was stopped at the side of the road, its head down, its back hunched, its rider squatted on the ground at its head. So that's what burn-out looks like, he thought. Soon, they passed another horse, this one walking slowly, its rider walking also. Then they passed Simone and the Dandy. In spite of himself he felt a twinge of excitement.

"Hey-hey-hey," he called to his horse, and his spirit soared even as his ears began to buzz.

Five miles to go. Jordy was feeling faint. He clutched a section of mane to steady himself. He was aware of another horse ahead of him but he couldn't see it. It took all his strength and concentration to stay in the saddle.

Hey-hey-hey, he sang inside his head. Stay on. Stay on. He could hear humming in his ears. He didn't know the horse ahead of him was Abdul al Aba, or that it was leading. Instead he saw again the horse he'd seen almost a year ago in the blizzard. Feathers fluttered from the back of the rider's long black hair. In the air above him, a gathering host of leather-fringed horsemen was stirring up the wind. Their chanting filled the sky and made the earth tremble.

The rider looked back at Jordy. He beckoned. Jordy urged his horse towards it. "Siksika," the rider said. A war whoop filled the air.

Grandfather Speckledhawk was perched on top of Albert's truck. When he stretched, he could see over the top of Jawarski's fifty-thousand-dollar multi-horse van out to the prairie.

"What's goin' on?" Albert called up to him.

"Can't tell."

"Look through these." He tossed up binoculars.

"It's Jordy!" whispered the old man after a while.

"What?"

"Jordy! He's comin' in!"

There was his grandson, moving up on the Arab until, head to head, the two horses broke into a run. Stride for stride, the animals matched each other in courage and strength. Joe felt his heart fill with pride, a clear, unmarred pride. He let out a whoop of joy.

The two horses came to the finish together. They were surrounded by officials and crews and cameramen, everyone talking at once. Jordy slid off the mare into Albert's waiting arms. The vet checked each horse. Jordy slumped against Albert's paunch.

"The kid won," somebody said.

"How's that?"

"Started ten minutes after, finished with Jawarski. The mare won."

A camera crew rushed up to Jordy. A microphone was shoved under his nose.

"Great race, Jordy. Tell us about this horse, Jordy. . . . You got her off the prairie, that right?"

"Yeah." He grinned.

"It says here her name's Horse, that right?"

"No."

"What's her name?"

"Siksika!"

"What's that?"

Albert beamed. He wrapped a big arm around the boy and hugged him.

"Blackfoot," said the chief and his eyes shone brightly. "The name means Blackfoot!"

If you liked this story then why not look out for other Kelpies. There are dozens of stories to choose from : ghosts, spy stories, animals and the countryside, witches, mysteries and secrets, adventures and many more. Kelpie paperbacks are available from all good bookshops.

For your free Kelpie badge and complete catalogue please send a stamped addressed envelope to: Margaret Ritchie (K.C.B.), Canongate Publishing Ltd., 17 Jeffrey Street, Edinburgh EH1 1DR.